P.J.'s Bookstore
235 Piney Forest Rd.
Danville, Va. 24540
(434) 799-0381

Betting Hearts

By Dee Tenorio

A Samhain Publishing, Ltd. publication.

Samhain Publishing, Ltd.
2932 Ross Clark Circle, #384
Dothan, AL 36301
www.samhainpublishing.com

First Samhain Publishing, Ltd. electronic publication: June 2006
First Samhain Publishing, Ltd. print publication: September 2006

Dedication

For Barbara Alvarado Hernandez: Without you, there literally aren't words.

For Alan: You are the reason there are heroes.

For Moo: For making my dreams real.

For Pet, Rae, X, Anna & Wax: For putting up with more than you should have longer than anyone else would have. You deserve medals.

You are the reason I never quit.

Special thanks to Angie, for clearing the chaff.

Chapter One

"If I asked you to have sex with me, would you do it?"

Not precisely the question Burke Halifax expected to hear when opening his door at three-thirty in the morning. Nor did he expect to find CB Bishop there, looking like a drowned rat.

A *drunk* drowned rat.

"CB?" He scrubbed at his eye with the heel of his hand. "What the hell are you talking about?"

She swayed, the yellow light of the outside lamp turning her sallow while wind and water pelted her from all sides. "Remember when you used to call me Cass?"

She woke me to ask that dumb-ass question? "How much have you had to drink?"

"Not enough." Her shoulders hunched in the pouring rain. She had to be dead drunk not to come under the eaves. She lifted her chin—*God, I hate when she does that*—asking louder, "Do you remember?"

"Yeah, I remember. It's been years. No one calls you Cass any more." Not if they wanted to keep their arms. Cassandra Bishop had a left hook like Mike Tyson when she was good and riled. He should know, he taught her when she was eight.

"You never answered my first question," she accused, apparently satisfied with his grudging answer.

She damn well better be. She wasn't getting another one. "Are you coming in from the rain or what?"

"You wouldn't, would you?"

"CB—"

"My name is *Cassandra!*"

Burke's temper rose. She woke him out of a sound sleep in the middle of the night to argue with him in the rain about whether or not he was in the mood? Hell, no, he wasn't in the mood and he told her as much.

She nodded without emotion. "Thanks. S'what I thought." She turned around, leaving as mysteriously as she arrived.

Burke slammed the door, intent on heading back to his warm bed and his dream of a cool blonde. Two steps later, he woke up enough to realize he'd let a drunken woman go out into a rainstorm to drive herself home. Swearing, he went back to the front door, rushing out in boxers and bare feet. When she was sober, he had every intention of killing her.

CB's car—a wicked black '82 Z-28 he helped her restore himself—was nowhere to be found. Just as he was imagining all their hard work wrapped around a phone poll, he saw her trudging under a street lamp half a block away.

One thing he could say about a drunk CB, she didn't move quick.

Burke, now as drenched as she was, ran down the street at full speed to catch her. She didn't respond to him at all. He grabbed her arm, spinning her around. She followed his lead, letting him haul her back to his house. It was a fairly clinical twenty minutes after that, if one discounted all the swearing Burke did while dragging her into his bathroom, stripping her down to her cotton underwear and shoving her head under warm water while she screamed. Satisfied she was as unhappy as he was, he turned the water hot to get the blue tinge off her and held her there no matter how much she fought him.

A man needed a bit of restitution after what she'd done.

He wrapped her in a towel, carried her to his guest room and dumped her there on the bed with about as much care as he'd give to a sack of potatoes. If she wanted blankets, she damn well had to get under them herself. He'd done all he was required as a friend. Still in a huff, Burke dried off, more than ready to go back to his bed, his blankets and his dreamy blonde. If CB wanted to stay alive in the morning, the blonde damn well better still be there.

Cass didn't feel like herself when she woke up. She felt like a smashed bug. Fitting, since she'd intended to get smashed, but at the time she'd been hoping to die from it.

The day before had gone reasonably well. Sunny overhead, a cool enough breeze to keep the windows on her landscaping truck down and hum along to the music on the radio while she ran errands. The last stop before heading back to the nursery was The One Stop Bar & Grille to give an estimate. It should have been an easy twenty minutes of work and possibly a sandwich. Instead…well, things got bizarre.

First, she needed to meet Henry, the manager, inside instead of along the perimeter where he wanted her to redesign. No big deal. Until she saw Luke Hanson walk in and *The Twilight Zone* music began playing in her head. Handsome, confident, swaggering ex-fiancé, Luke. Not-seen-in-more-than-a-year Luke. Hoped-never-to-see-again Luke. More correctly Luke and his *date*. The date wasn't the problem; Cass even expected a blonde if this horrible moment were ever to happen.

She never expected a woman.

That was about when she decided to get drunk enough to forget the entire day. Unfortunately, she was still a few kegs shy of oblivion.

Feeling the cold air on her skin, she realized she was a few garments shy of dressed as well.

Peeling open an eye with one almost cooperative hand, she looked around the room. From the warm tan paint and the portrait of a cowboy with his pony on the wall, Cass realized she was in the only safe place in Rancho de Cielo—Burke's house. How she got here was a mystery, but not one of any importance. No one would be stupid enough to take her to her father's house in her condition. Eddie Bishop might not pay attention to much, but he'd yell the rafters down if she had to be poured into her bed. The same could be said of Burke, however she had the advantage of ignoring him with little to no guilt. That is, until he opened the door to the bedroom, piercing sunlight at his back. She let her eyelid snap into place and groaned.

"Mind telling me what you thought you were doing last night?"

Cass flinched at the familiar sound of his gravelly voice. Some men sounded smoky, some men spoke rough. Burke spoke with a lazy rumble and grind she could only compare to mountain lions. This morning, he might well have been a garbage disposal ripping up quarters.

"What's the matter, *Cassandra*? Am I talking too loud?"

Cass rolled over, belatedly realizing she was still above the blankets. She pulled the fabric away to dig out the pillow and covered her head. The movement hurt something awful, but at least she couldn't hear him anymore. "Go away."

He lifted the corner of the pillow high enough to shed light on her face. "What *Cassandra*? Couldn't hear you."

"Go away!" Hearing her own voice was worse than hearing his, but she'd do it. Even pain was better than Burke in lecture mode.

"I would, but I thought you might want some breakfast."

Something smelled revoltingly like fried eggs, way too close to her face for the future integrity of Burke's pristine white sheets.

"Are you wearing your boots?" she asked, slowly and softly, hoping the impact inside her skull wouldn't be horrific. It was.

"Why?" Good. He *should* sound suspicious.

"Because if you don't take it away, I'm going to enjoy throwing up all over them." Might even do it twice.

"In that case, no, I'm not."

Bastard. "Leave me alone, Burke." Why wouldn't he let her die in peace? She wanted to whimper, she wanted to scream. She settled for under-the-pillow dignity.

"I would, CB, I really would…but it's not often I see a woman in cotton undies anymore. I can't remember the last time I saw a set of grannies in that shade of military gray. I think it's starting to do something for me."

Both her eyes opened now. Sitting up faster than was wise, she gathered the dark blue towel from its tangle beneath her belly and clutched it in front of her. Stomach lurching, hair probably on end, God only knew what kind of blotches on her face, Cass knew she was a human rendition of ugly at its worst. All the while he stood there, perfectly pressed in a blue chambray shirt and jeans neat enough to have never been worn before. God hated her. No other explanation available. Why else would He give her a friend as put together as Burke Halifax? She refused outright to give him any extra points for combed hair that actually looked combed, his wide brilliant smile or devil-sexy face. No one got points for good genetics.

"I hate you," she growled, which only seemed to amuse him more.

"Funny." He dared to step closer, shifting the tray against his hip. "Last night you were trying to have sex with me."

She eyed him, glad she was hung over enough to be truly baleful. "How much did *you* drink?"

He laughed, probably because he knew it made her head reverberate. "Not enough to give you what you wanted."

Cass knew he didn't say it to be cruel. She was over-sensitive right now. Still, it hurt and his blue eyes flickered when he realized it. She wiped her cheek with the back of her hand, hoping to make him think it was just her face being contrary instead of a real emotion.

He must have bought it because he shrugged and put the tray on the bureau before sitting next to her. Clean transition from brother-like friend to father-like friend completed. She rolled her eyes and prepared for the lecture. Well, she would have. They were too dry to roll.

"You haven't pulled a stunt like this since your freshman year in college. What happened last night?"

Lying wouldn't get her anywhere. It was probably all over their tiny town already. The only thing faster than the gossip in Rancho Del Cielo was lightening. Even then, it was a close race.

She let the air out of her lungs. "I ran into Luke."

His expression softened and understanding flooded his eyes. Except, he didn't understand. He couldn't. "Aw, Cassie."

She didn't want his pity, he only called her Cassie when he felt bad for her. Usually when Luke was involved. "It doesn't matter."

It didn't. Luke was the past. A mistake. A long, miserable, life-staining mistake.

"I know how you felt about the guy, but it's been nearly a year since he…" Burke let the sentence trail away. Everyone in town did that. Referred to her embarrassment instead of directly discussing it, like it would be any easier to deal with that way.

"Since he called off the wedding," she stated clearly, watching him wince at the bluntness. "I'm not a little kid. You can say it in front of me."

"Well if you're not a kid, you should know you can't go getting this upset every time you see him."

"I don't plan to," she snapped. "You're not my father, Burke. Stop trying to teach me dating etiquette. It's not like you know the first thing about dealing with relationships. The longest one you ever had was one that time you gave the girl a ride home."

He gave her a glare and harrumphed. Burke for *That's not the point.*

"It doesn't matter," she grumbled again, looking down at her hands and trying to smooth the towel over more of her body. She didn't know why. Burke wasn't looking at her body. He was staring at her face, waiting for elaboration. He never did like facing a situation without all the details, important or not. "I figure Luke's cleared out of town. I won't be seeing him again."

"Yeah, why not?" He reached for the coffee mug off and took a sip.

"Because after I broke his nose I told him to get out and never come back."

He sputtered, barely catching himself from sending a spray across his beloved white Berber carpet. His eyes really were a vivid blue, when they were this wide and she could get such a good look at them.

He wiped his mouth with a slash of his hand. "You *what?*"

"I broke his nose." She looked around the room. Anything but look directly at him. Wasn't that some kind of rule at the zoo? *Don't make eye contact with the rampaging animal.* "Where are my clothes?"

"Back up. *Why* did you break his nose?"

"I couldn't hit the blonde he was with. What is it with you men and your cute little blondes?" Cass stretched out a leg to see if the ground was stable enough to stand up on.

"I thought Luke was…um…more inclined toward big, burly blondes now."

Isn't that a polite way of saying it?

"Nope. His tastes haven't changed as much as we thought they did. This was a tiny, petite little blonde with big blue eyes, big red lips and big thirty-eight double-Ds." Cass trembled to her feet. She looked down to her own breasts. The only D she could use came from the word "Depressing".

"But if he was with a woman—"

"He's not gay." Cass braced her hand on the bureau. So far so good. Both legs working now. "He only said it so he wouldn't have to marry me. He's going to marry Miss Grand Tetons. The only reason he was in town was to introduce her to his parents, the weasel. He thought since I'd most likely be down at Shaky Jakes, they'd go to The One Stop."

Rancho Del Cielo could only boast three restaurants. Shaky Jakes, a bar and burger joint; The One Stop, a fancy new place designed for lady's lunches; and a McDonald's by the freeway exit on the way out of town. Most everyone went to Shaky Jakes, where May Belle Butner served up her famous burgers and a hotline to all the town gossip. The other two places survived on tourism.

Usually Cass wouldn't be found dead in a place like The One Stop. Any other day she would never have seen him.

"Aww, Cassie."

"I'm going to go soak in your tub. Leave my clothes by the door, will you?" Cass made herself walk out of the square room and head toward Burke's decadent bathroom. She was going to soak in his Jacuzzi tub and she was going to hope and pray he didn't say one more thing about last night.

Watching CB wobble her way out of the guest room as if her entire life depended on the scrap of pride she had left made Burke angrier than he would ever admit to her.

He never did like Luke Hanson. He especially hadn't liked him when CB showed off her engagement ring two years ago. At the time, he figured it was because Luke Hanson's arrival in RDC—way back when she was in the seventh grade—caused her to leave the circle of himself and her brother to play football with the new, cute quarterback. He hadn't liked being replaced, although he knew she'd be back. He simply never expected her to be back so often...

It never made much sense to Burke, why Luke strung her along as the years went by. Or why Cass put up with it. She was smart. Sometimes she was even reasonable. And Luke Hanson was a moron. It never added up right. What was the attraction? Why did they play the make-up/break-up game over and over again? Some months they'd hang out like best buddies—in high school they even called it dating. Then Cass would be left broken-hearted while Luke made up for lost time with the cheerleaders. Only Burke seemed to notice their break ups coincided with the football season. As star quarterback, Luke had his pick every year of the girls. He never once chose Cass.

When he didn't get a football scholarship as everyone expected, Luke managed to fully descend into a disconsolate schmuck. Back he came to Cass like a sniveling weasel. She dragged him to community college with her when she could have gone to State without him. Month after month, year after year, until they both had a business degree. Luke's was in a frame in his father's house, next to the sports trophies. CB's was in the twice expanded and still growing nursery and landscaping company her father founded. This year, she'd added a florist section to the success.

Ever since grade school, Luke had been taking and benefiting from his relationship with CB. Marrying her was going to be his reward to her, and again, only Burke saw it for what it was. The leech meant to suck her dry for the rest of their lives. The thought alone had been enough to enrage him. Seeing it happen wasn't something he could stomach, either.

He freely admitted he got in the way of the nuptials whenever possible. Subtlety not being his thing, Burke tromped his way through every detail he could find, looking for a way to create a wedge. He started with simple things, flooding her with questions, drowning her in minutiae he knew she didn't have the patience for—when did she want to do it, where would they honeymoon, shouldn't they get a place to live first? That alone bought a few months filled with pamphlets and brochures she grew less and less interested in reading. The coup de grâce was asking if she wanted a big traditional wedding like her parents. Her temper kicked into overdrive when Luke complained she didn't need any fuss. He'd rather go to a justice of the peace and get it over with.

The words "get it over with" were what bothered Burke. As if the man were getting inoculations instead of a bride. But it did allow Burke to swallow his discomfort at openly wrecking her relationship with as big a sledgehammer as he could find. He was being a good friend, protecting her before she made the biggest mistake of her life. Protecting her, after all, was what his entire life was about.

Two weeks before a wedding even Burke couldn't push back any further, CB showed up on his doorstep with a letter and a stunned look on her face. Luke had left town, explaining he'd been lying to her, to everyone. He had planned to marry her in a last ditch attempt to ignore the truth—he was gay. The letter went on to say he was moving to LA where his looks would get him work and his life choices wouldn't hold him back.

Burke had to work hard not to smile when he read that letter.

Word got around Rancho Del Cielo like wildfire, although no one seemed to remember who they heard it from first. People whispered at first, then joked, then claimed to have known all along ole Luke was "thatta way". Of course, people pitied CB for being used. Luke's parents apologized to her, taking it upon themselves to pay for the wedding plans, and CB's beautiful wedding dress went into a plastic bag in the back of her closet. Eventually life went back to normal, exactly the way Burke knew it would.

CB continued working for her father's business. Burke continued to rebuild custom cars. They went back to their Friday night poker games with the guys. It was a happy life. For a whole year, CB had done fine. She smiled, she laughed, she ate with gusto and played every game like it was war. He certainly had no complaints.

Until last night.

Luke Hanson being the one and only thing that could screw up his world didn't surprise Burke. He'd have to be blind, deaf, dumb and stupid to miss that. He just hoped the lying, cheating, snake in the grass had better sense than to stick around after messing with it this time, because Burke had no intention of letting the little bugger get away with it again.

Burke Halifax did not deserve a tub like this.

Cass sank into the bubble-filled, obsidian pool, the jets quietly blasting her body, removing her physical aches. She looked out the triple windows to the high fronds of various plants and greenery she had planted to give some semblance of modesty to the bather. Not that Burke had a modest bone in his body. She was sure she would have seen it once or twice over the twenty-two years he'd been her best friend. She'd seen nearly everything else.

Burke was three years older and her brother's classmate when they met. She was six, he was nine. Her brother was constantly trying to get rid of her, but Burke seemed to like her spunky tenacity. There were times he'd play with her more often than Hayne. Of course, Hayne wasn't as good at marbles as she was. He couldn't pull a ball for a home run until high school—she finally taught him how—and he had this pesky thing for girls at a young age. Burke knew what was really important: baseball cards. Part of Cass's charm, she knew, was she had a bigger collection than him.

Hayne had other friends, but by the time Cass was a teen, she only had Burke. The girls didn't like her—something about how she'd get them dirty, *giggle, giggle*—and the boys were intimidated. That was what Burke said anyway. When she was thirteen, Burke's word was law.

Cass smiled wickedly despite her headache. Things were certainly different now.

These days, she kind of enjoyed making up her own mind. Burke always put in his two cents—usually closer to a buck-fifty—but he respected her enough to let her take care of herself.

Except whenever she was dating Luke.

At that unhappy thought, Cass's closed eyes fluttered.

Instead of thinking back on those idyllic days when the town sweetheart had eyes only for her, Cass remembered the night before. Turning away from the manager of the One Stop and the polished black oak bar with its shiny gold rail to see Luke waltzing in, a brilliant smile on his perfect face…and the human equivalent of a Pomeranian skittering behind him on platform stilettos.

Cass had stared in awe as Luke followed the maitre d' to a table, walking right past her. She apparently blended right into the dark garden atmosphere because Luke never noticed her. Not until he leaned over to kiss his date, who made such a high-pitched squeal of delight it should have shattered the water glasses. He must have spotted her out of the corner of his eye, because he pulled back and scrambled to his feet, nearly sending the blonde toppling out of her chair.

"CB!"

"Luke." She had a heck of a time saying his name without a shotgun in her hand.

"Funny seeing you here." Because it wasn't like she lived there or anything.

Cass nodded. "Funny seeing you with a girl."

"Yeah, well," Luke replied, his face reddening. "About that—"

"Is she getting a sex change operation?"

"Excuse me?" the Pomeranian asked, eyes wide enough to pop.

Cass gave the woman a fleeting glance. "I would, honey, but that hairdo can't be forgiven."

"Hey, now," Luke took a step forward and put a hand on the Pom's shoulder. "Don't go insulting Sally!"

"Sally?" she asked. "*Sally?*" Was he serious? He left her with a note—a got-damned *note!*—saying he was gay and now he showed up with a *woman?* Luke started backing away from the table as CB advanced on him. "What are you doing with a *Sally?* I thought you went off to find yourself a *Steve.* Or a *Mark.* Even a *Billy. Sallys* were specifically off your list of preferences, remember? Or did the boobs bigger than her head change your mind?"

"There's a very good reason for this, CB. A very good explanation for all of this."

"So spill it."

Luke moved his head to look for Sally, still seated at the table behind Cass. "Well, did you look at her?"

Before she even realized what she was doing, Luke was soaring through the air and crashing on a table. It collapsed beneath him while Cass shook her hand out.

"You broke my nose!" he roared from the floor.

"You deserved it," she mumbled, making sure her knuckles weren't bleeding. A little skinned, aching like hell. Hitting Luke felt a lot like punching a rock.

Luke covered his bloody nose with his hand, glaring at her. Sally rushed over with a wad of napkins and a few whimpers of terror. "You see? *This* is why I didn't want to marry you, CB!" he yelled, making no motion to get up. "You have no sense of civility!"

"And pretending you're homosexual reeks of it?"

"It was the only way to break it off without getting my damn nose broken! You got less control than a fricken' bronco." Sally helped him to his feet, but Luke continued to yell nasally at Cass. "Everyone always said I should just throw a saddle on your ass. Maybe I shouldda listened. You might have figured out how to act for once."

"Yeah, yeah, yeah. God forbid you forget anything your idiot friends say about me. If I was such a pain, why were you always on your hands and knees trying to get me back?" Okay, hands and knees was a little bit of a stretch, but it fit at the time.

"'Cause I'd get sick and tired of putting up with women who want you to do everything for them all the time. They spend all your time and all your money making themselves look good. Truth is, CB, you were easy. Like being with one of the guys. I never had to do anything but be there. Hell, sometimes not even that.

"I can put up with all the other crap women do. It's worth it not to get beat up by your girlfriend all the time. I want a woman who makes me feel like a man. Not one who makes me feel like a wimp. So I got the hell out and found one. I only came home to tell my parents the truth. I tried to make things easy on you by taking the blame, but not anymore!"

Cass tensed, rage held onto by a thread. "Is that some sort of threat?"

"Maybe." Luke grabbed another wad of napkins out of the dispenser on the nearest table. "Yeah, yeah it is!"

"Luke, I swear by all that's holy, if you don't get out of this town—and I mean quick—I'll break a helluva lot more than your nose."

He shook his head, snide as he stumbled to stand. "See, you can't even make threats like a girl. You gotta beat people up. Being with *you* is being gay. Come on, Sally."

Luke shoved past her, leaning heavily on Sally and her wobbly shoes. Cass didn't remember much more than that. A fuzzy recollection of telling Henry to send her a bill for the table. She couldn't say for sure. Somehow or another, she'd arrived at Shaky Jakes and kept the tequila coming, no matter how much May Belle tried to get her to slow down.

Now, sitting in Burke's tub, Cass brought her wet hand to her pounding forehead. No amount of alcohol could erase Luke's words. Or the truth behind them. She sank into the water, glad the swirling bubbles would erase any and all proof of her tears.

"Hey! You awake?" Burke stared down at CB, trying to decide if she was conscious or not. He really didn't want to get wet hauling her out.

Her eyelids lifted and he suddenly got the impression she was mad. Might have had something to do with her splashing to an upright position and screeching unintelligibly. *Damn, there goes the plan to stay dry.*

"Brought you something fresh to wear."

"What are you *doing* in here?"

"Didn't I just tell you?"

She crossed her arms over her chest. "I'm naked, Burke!"

"So?"

That was the wrong thing to say. Her face turned a shade of red that lit up the sprinkle of freckles on her cheeks and made those green eyes glow like something unholy. "So? *So!* "

And here comes more screeching…

She didn't disappoint. She continued calling him names as she groped around for a towel, but it was out of her reach. That's what she got for hijacking a man's bathtub. He got an evil eye or two before she finally gave up trying to stay in the bubbles and get the towel at the same time. "Will you grab it for me?"

"Sorry, didn't catch that. You might want to repeat it in…what language did you say I spoke? Backwoods Redneckese?"

"Just get me the damn towel!"

He shrugged. "Get it yourself."

For a second, she seemed to pout. "If I do, you'll see me."

"Seen it all before. What do *you* have that's special?"

There it was again, the flinch of her eye. When did CB start getting sensitive? She'd always had the skin of a rhino. Was he supposed to start worrying over everything he said to her? No doubt, Hansen had to be behind this, too. Whatever was wrong with her, she didn't feel like talking about it because she went right back to being mad, mouth in a cranky little rainbow of gloom.

"Fine." She stood, bubbles dripping off her, and reached for the towel, having to bend down and secure one hand on the edge of the tub to keep from slipping. She covered herself as quickly as she could, dunking half the towel in soapy water before flouncing her way out of the tub, past him and out the bathroom door like Sheba, queen of the sandbox. He couldn't quite say where she went afterward.

He was too busy trying to breathe.

Naked women. He knew he'd seen them before. Plenty of them. Somehow, he'd never seen one like that. Bronzed arms and shoulders slowly lightened into pale, pale cream. Not a single freckle there or there or…he swallowed, *there*.

Maybe it was the water sluicing over her. That had to be it. How many other women were lucky enough to be backlit by golden sunshine glittering down their sudsy curves the first time they were seen in the buck?

Somehow, breathing wasn't getting easier.

Where did she get off having breasts anyway? He'd never noticed them before, and a set like that would have demanded his attention. Even on CB. And who the hell gave her permission to have an ass like *that*? Did her brother know about this?

He turned around, not quite sure why he expected her to still be in the doorway. He wasn't even angry about the big sploshes of water on the tiled floor. He wasn't anything but… No, he wasn't aroused. Not by Little Miss Mud Pie. He dropped down onto the black commode, running a hand over his face, pretending to himself he wasn't uncomfortable in his jeans.

Hayne—the brother who should have warned him about this— would kill him. Theirs was an agreement from ages ago. To hang out with CB without supervision, he could never see her as anything worth getting a hard-on over. Ever. The more women he dated and dropped, unable to feel anything for them beyond boredom, the more Hayne invoked the sacred oath. No hard-ons. Which was fine. The good buddy below had obliged without question. Until now.

No, not now. Not ever. He wasn't aroused. He was shocked. Surprised. Disturbed. Yes, that was a better word. Extremely, extremely disturbed. He took a deep breath.

So, CB had…feminine attributes. He supposed she was allowed. If he thought about it, he should have noticed when he stripped her the night before. Of course, she was still in her underwear and he *was* pretty mad. So mad he hadn't seen her pert, strawberry colored nipples. Not that those should bother him. Everyone had nipples. *He* had nipples. Nipples were a good thing. Tasty, sweet things…

Damn it, Hayne *was* going to kill him.

"Burke, where are those clothes?" she called from one of the bedrooms.

"In my—" He stopped to cough, wondering where the taut, higher pitch in his voice came from. "Grab something from my drawers!"

That was *not* some kind of Freudian slip.

"Sweats okay?"

Sure, sweating was good. He was sweating right now. "Perfect. Look, I'm gonna…I have to…I'm…I'll be back."

"Wait, if you're leaving you can give me a lift back to my place!"

"No!" Catching himself, he walked out of the bathroom and nearly ran into her in the hallway.

She was still in that damn black towel, scowling up at him like a kitten unable to figure out how to get up a tree. "You okay?"

"Fine, I'm just not headed that way, and you're best out of sight." *Out of sight, out of mind.*

"But—"

"Relax, I'll be right back."

"But—"

Rather than think about one more but—or worse, remember getting too good a look at one—Burke grabbed his keys from the dish and rushed out of his house.

Chapter Two

Just when she thought the man might have a brain in his head, he went and proved her wrong. Cass pulled Burke's too long sweatpants up over her hips, allowing the elastic binding at the ends to cup the fabric under her feet like ready-made slippers. She would have put on the matching sweatshirt, but if Burke could get a look at her naked, she could steal his favorite T-shirt.

The dark purple cotton smelled like the cedar from his dresser, a scent she had to admit she associated with him. Regardless of his jackass tendencies, the smell was comforting and she willingly wrapped herself up in it. He'd never know anyway, so there.

She hadn't figured out yet what happened earlier. He said he'd seen more than one naked female body and hers was the last one on earth to stun him. Why the big frazzle? Maybe he was still upset about Luke returning? Well, why not? She was.

Of course, Burke upset meant he did one of two things; beat someone up or worked on a car. Since Luke was already sufficiently beaten—not to mention gone—she figured he went to the shop. Good, she didn't want him around during a hangover anyway. Burke was only good for two things: whining to and playing poker with. He wasn't bad at cooking either, but he had too many rules about eating. Not in front of the television, not in a hurry and not from the drive-thru. At least he didn't begrudge her pizza from time to time.

Restlessly, she got back up and went into his kitchen. Maybe he had something salty. Hangover or not, her stomach could only be held off for so long. Thankfully, he had pretzels all set for tonight's poker game.

The game was a weekly institution for them, something they started back in high school. Even Luke had to come if he wanted her time. For a while, it was only she, Burke and Hayne. Later Sel Panyon, another teen buddy, came back to town and he edged into the game. Then he brought his wife, Alice, who had a poker face even Cass envied. Before they knew it, there were three others who rotated in and out of the game on any given week. Made for some rousing Friday nights.

Cass grabbed the bag and promised herself to bring a replacement when she came back to play. If Burke ever gave her a ride home. Geez, you'd think a guy could bang out his frustrations a little faster. Well, until he got back she was going to lay all over his furniture, eat wherever she wanted and leave crumbs on his immaculate leather couch. Teach him to take his time. Settling into the seat, she ripped open the bag only to be interrupted at the chime of the doorbell.

Just my luck. She snitched two pretzels, popping them past her lips before hustling to the door.

The last person Cass expected there was Luke Hanson. Her jaws crunched down on the tiny bread sticks. If God was kind, she didn't look like she'd stuffed a hanger in her mouth. Luke snickered. She thought. Hard to tell, what with his face behind the gauze covering him from bridge to upper lip. All she could go on was the plunger popping sound from beneath it all.

"How did I know I'd find you here?" His slow drawl lost something important without the ability to stick his consonants.

Where else would I be? "You bought a brain in LA?"

He managed to smirk at her, looking her up and down until his gaze turned into a leer. "I can totally see your nips through your shirt."

Cass crossed her arms. Not because she cared if he took a look at her breasts or not—though the thought made her skin twitch. No, she did it to keep her hands pressed firmly to her sides. Why bother swinging? He wouldn't feel it if she punched him again, not through all the gauze. She leaned against the door instead, feigning nonchalance. "Hope you enjoyed it, you'll never see them again."

"Thank God for small miracles." Was his smile always this mean? What exactly did she love about this guy? "Real small."

It would be nice to wrap her hands around his neck. Better yet, ram her knee into his breadbasket and leave him wheezing on Burke's porch, but by the time the thought finished playing in her imagination, she was bored. Gauzed or perfect, he just wasn't worth her time. She flicked her fingers at him, shooing him off the stoop. "Goodbye, Luke."

He grabbed the hem of Burke's T-shirt to keep her from escaping. "Not so fast, Bazooka Jane."

Cass swiped the fabric out of his hands, her hand fisting to strike. Maybe just one more broken bone...

Hands raised, Luke let her go. "Can't leave without your invite, can you?"

"My what?" She forced her fingers to relax.

Luke extended his hand with a small white card. It was one of those pretty invitations with gold embossing and edges torn professionally to look feathered. The kind she wanted for her wedding but *he* complained were too expensive. "It's for you. I can't tell you how much we want you to be there."

He flicked it at her, the corner poking her in the empty valley between her breasts before fluttering to the ground with a whisper. "See you there."

She was still staring at it when he walked away.

♥ ♥ ♥

"A little early for you to be drinking, isn't it, Burke?"

He hunched over the beer glass, giving May Belle Butner what he hoped was an evil eye. Since he was preparing to down his second beer in ten minutes, he figured he had a pretty good one. But May Belle had probably seen better. "No, it's not."

"First CB is in here getting bombed, now you. Something we should know about?" We *being the entire town of Rancho Del Cielo, of course.*

"What I want to know is how CB got to my house last night."

"I told Jimmy to take her home. I guess he's got peculiar ideas where that is." She shrugged, her Shirley Temple blonde curls bouncing with indifference. She wasn't about to apologize for her husband—not that Jimmy ever needed her to. "She tell you about Luke?"

At one in the afternoon, Shaky Jake's wasn't particularly busy, but Burke heartily wished it was. He didn't want to talk about Luke or CB or anything else. He wanted to have his beer and pretend he didn't see anything worth looking at. Unfortunately, May Belle could sniff a bit of gossip the way bloodhounds found invisible trails.

"I can tell by that glare she did. I wasn't much happier seeing him back in town either, but what am I supposed to do? Business is business, I guess."

Burke frowned. "What business?"

May Belle picked up a towel and started drying glasses. "Turns out Luke's decided to get married here at home. His mother called me not ten minutes ago to ask if I could do the catering. We're working out the details later."

"He *what?*" Burke slammed his glass mug down hard enough to slosh half the beer over his hand.

May Belle didn't bat an eye at his volume or the mess. "Even someone as dumb as Luke doesn't need four hours in the emergency room to think up something vengeful. Too bad, too, because his little fiancée is actually sweet—"

"I don't care if she gives you diabetes, May, you can't cater that wedding."

She raised a shaped eyebrow. "You gonna pay me not to?"

"What do you think it's going to do to CB if he gets married here?"

May Belle shrugged, picking up a new glass to dry. "Probably not much, seeing as how she's glad to be free of him."

Burke shook his head. CB played a good bluff, but he knew better than most how hard she took losing the pretty boy. He was surprised May Belle fell for it, though. She had the sharpest eye in town. "We can't let him embarrass her this way."

"Burke, honey, CB can take care of herself. You taught her how, remember?"

He grumbled into what was left of his beer. "The point is he's doing it to rub her face in it and you're helping him."

"You look like a grumpy four-year-old. Stop whining. If you don't want it to happen, go talk to Luke. I got a business to run."

"Like Luke's going to listen to *me*."

May gave him a steamy look. "You're a good-looking man. Play on his...masculine side."

His disgust only made her laugh. "You're a sick woman, May Belle."

"And you're taking up space in my bar. Go home, go work on a car or something. Better yet, go talk to CB. I'll bet money if *you* didn't know anything about this yet, neither does she."

A whole host of words his mother would scrub his mouth out for fought for first dibs getting out of his mouth. Why didn't he think of that? Hanson might not be smart, but he was fast. No doubt he'd take first opportunity to rub this in her face. Burke jumped off the stool, calling behind him to put the bill on his tab. Eight minutes later he entered the house hoping to hear absolutely nothing. Instead he heard the thing he dreaded more than anything on earth.

Singing.

With one off-key, high-decibel, off-time note, he knew he was already too late. It wasn't right what CB could do to Garth Brooks. He shuddered every time she tried to attempt "Thunder Rolls". Especially bad, not only was she singing, she was suspiciously sniffing and gasping into skipped words. She was also nearly a whole line behind.

He headed into the kitchen, where the white CD player was failing to drown her out. He hit the stop button and pushed open the back door. He found her exactly where he expected; in the flowerbeds on her knees, her hands sunk into the still muddy earth between his rosebushes. Whenever she was upset, she tried to sing and till the entire earth single-handedly. She didn't abandon her task, continuing to turn over the dirt like an earthworm gone wrong.

"Garth threatened to sue last time, remember?"

No response.

"So did the neighbors."

Silence.

"Cassie?"

Then he heard the most awful thing. A full blown sob. Her shoulders hitched and everything. He stood there, shocked to immobility while she lowered her head and cried. What finally made him realize this wasn't some horrible nightmare was when she picked up her hand to cover her face.

"CB, no!"

She jumped, startled by his voice, plopping her rump on his thick grass and setting her elbows on her parted knees. Mud clumped to her fingers, falling in chunks between her feet. Her hair was still wet from her bath, rippling and unruly, strays in all directions, hanks dried into strings around her face. Those big green eyes of hers glistened miserably at him as tears poured over her spiked lashes.

God, why not shove a stake through my gut, Cassie?

"Honey, it isn't that bad."

"He's *marrying* her!" Brand new sobs bubbled out of her while she tried to say something else, but the lump in her throat seemed to keep her from making any intelligible noises.

"I heard."

"He-he-he-"

Burke stifled a groan. This was going to take a while. She wasn't this goopy when Luke left her practically at the altar. He grabbed the hose and brought it over to her, kissing off the rest of his day. She extended her hands at his gesture. He turned on the spray, sending mud dripping off them. Once she was reasonably clean, he helped her to her feet and led her back into the house.

She stopped crying by the time he got her to the couch, thank God, but she curled up on a blanket and turned away from him, which wasn't an improvement. He let her stay there, long enough to start some coffee. He carried in two mugs, one sweet and creamy the way she liked. She hadn't moved an inch and she didn't twitch at the scent of the coffee. Bad sign.

The white square of paper caught his eye when he put her mug on the coffee table. He tilted his head to inspect it, finding the gold-embossed pattern of two swans forming a heart with their necks.

A wedding invitation.

Cass knew it was stupid to be this upset over someone like Luke. Actually, it wasn't Luke bothering her. It was that he was right. How there weren't little horned ice skaters outside, she couldn't say, but it was true. She didn't know the first thing about being feminine. Being a girl. Being a wife. Worse, she was never going to find out. Burke might be uncomfortable for a moment in his otherwise blithe existence, but dammit, she deserved to cry about it.

Sitting in a heap on Burke's couch, she could see her entire dismal eternity spreading out before her. Friday night poker games until she was as old as Ben Friedly, one of May Belle's infamous regulars down at Shaky Jakes. The man was eighty if he was a day and not one person in town remembered him being married, having a date or even liking a girl. Then again, no one but Ben remembered the Depression with any clarity either. The point, the one she could see in the not-so-distant horizon, was she'd already left her best chances behind her.

She was doomed to always be Little Miss Mud Pie, Burke's good-buddy-good-pal, Hayne's not-so-little sister, champion of the Annual Beer Guzzling Contest three years running. She couldn't sing, couldn't dance, couldn't date, couldn't cook, couldn't do her hair or her makeup, wouldn't know what to do at a baby shower—much less with a baby—and had never worn a pair of high heels in her life. She was going to spend eternity knowing the best she'd ever been able to scrounge as a boyfriend was Luke Hanson. That alone was depressing. The rest was gravy to boil in.

Busy dwelling in the bleak abyss of her future she didn't notice Burke picked up the invitation until he was reading it.

"This guy has no class at all," he grumbled.

"What, you don't think it's acceptable to cross out the vital information on your engraved wedding invitation to scribble corrections in the borders?" she asked through swollen sinuses. "I thought it was the *in* thing this year."

"He's only doing this to get back at you for breaking his nose."

She tossed him a sour look. "Thanks, Burke. Where would I be without you to point out the obvious?"

He shrugged, back to his reading. The next part was the real kicker. It was what sent Cass out to the backyard in the first place.

"CB—we'll understand if you can't make it. We know how hard it would be to find a tux in your size." Burke read, monotone, then inspected her from head to toe. "Why would a woman need a tux?"

"I'm only a technical woman." Cass held her still cold hands over her puffy eyes, sighing with relief. "I've got the equipment, I don't have a clue how to use it."

"Is *that* what he said?"

She appreciated his burgeoning anger, but really, who was he kidding? "Basically." She'd never tell him what Luke *actually* said.

"CB—"

She turned her head to face him. He had the scrunched frown on his face that didn't belong there this time and they both knew it. "He's right, Burke. Even Luke gets to be right once in a while. Everyone knows it. I'm an utter failure in the girl department. I don't deserve what little breast I have."

"Uh—"

She looked down at the slopes barely denting the shirt on her chest. "No one notices them anyway."

"Hon—"

"I mean, when was the last time *you* ever looked at them?"

Burke blinked at her as if she had pointed a loaded shotgun at his head.

She sighed. She probably had. Poor guy, he didn't deserve this. "Never mind."

At least he breathed again.

"I just…I wish I had something to offer a man."

"You have plenty to offer," he practically choked out. God, the only thing he did worse than bluffing was out and out lying.

"My landscaping business? Yeah, men fall all over themselves for women with green thumbs."

"You're being too hard on yourself." He tossed the card back on the table with disgust. It lay face up, the feathered edges catching her eye. What would it have been like, to mail some of those instead of the plain beige cards printed from her own computer? Put one in a photo album? Or let your kids touch it with gentle awe years and years later? She'd never find out. She'd never know what she was missing. Didn't that make it worse?

"I'm facing facts. I'm not girl material. I'm not wife material. I'm exactly what Luke said I was—one of the guys." So much of a guy he felt gay for being with her. Her chest tightened painfully, stomach clenching until she swore under her breath. "I need to accept it and move on."

"Cassie, the last thing on earth you should accept is the opinion of an ass like Luke Hanson. The man couldn't pour piss out of a boot with instructions on the heel. You really think *he* can make a judgment on what makes you a woman?"

Probably not, but it didn't take a genius to know she wasn't going to find a man interested in spending the rest of his life with her. Why would he bother? She wasn't attractive, wasn't sexy on her best day and had no interest in making anyone feel better about his hard day when she had one of her own. No one other than Burke, anyway. Which worked out. Odds were, he'd be the only man not blood-related to her staying with her till the day she died. She turned to him. "What do *you* think makes a woman feminine?"

He leaned back into the couch and pulled her feet onto his lap by her ankles. "I don't know. Looks aren't it though. All that's just training. You might not know all the girly magazine stuff, but you're a woman where it counts."

She wiggled her toes so he'd rub. "Yeah, where's that?"

"I don't know, CB." His palm took hold of her foot firmly, the heel of it pushing small circles against her arch. "Femininity is mystery, not an organ. You know it when you see it. You've got it in there. Somewhere."

Way to sound reassuring, Burke. "Sure I do." Right where he was rubbing if the tingles and urge to groan were any indication.

"You do," he insisted, ceasing the pressure from his hand.

She opened her eyes, ready to insist he get back to his work, and met his glare.

"I see it all the time."

She gaped. No one else in twenty-eight years had seen it, including her. Burke bowed his head, picking up the other foot to massage, signaling the topic closed.

She frowned. He couldn't say something like that and pretend there was nothing else to discuss. When did he see it? Why didn't he mention it? She wanted to see it. She hated looking in the mirror and seeing what Luke did. Couldn't he—

"No, Cassie." He didn't pick up his head, but she could feel the pressure on her instep change.

"You don't know what I was going to ask."

"I don't have to know. You're upset. You're hurt. Anything you think up right now is going to get you in a world of trouble. It always does."

Cass folded her arms and set her foot bouncing in time with her irritation.

He followed it with his hands for a moment before dropping them from her entirely. "Fine, but it's gonna be a bad idea."

"Think you could help me bring it out?"

He laughed, absently returning to his task, relief evident. "It's not a dinner tray."

"No, but…" An idea formed—an odd, fanciful, fascinating idea. Something Burke was guaranteed not to approve but sounded like exactly the right thing to do. "You said it's all in the training, right?"

Uh-oh. She could see him rethinking his laxity. His hands on her foot tightened, his back straightening with the scent of danger. She rushed to explain herself before he wigged out completely.

"You could teach me!" Oh, oh it'd be perfect. Wouldn't Luke's jaw fall off if she came into the church dressed to the nines and so sexy that every man in Rancho Del Cielo was overcome with desire?

"No, I couldn't!" He bumped her feet off his lap as if she'd caught fire.

Maybe she had. The idea had merit.

"Sure you could. You said you see my femininity all the time. You said—"

"I was trying to make you feel better."

"Were you lying?" The very real possibility brought her pause.

His discomfort started to resemble a blush. She never knew Burke's face was capable of reddening. "Uh…no, but CB—"

"Then you *can* do it!"

"No."

"Yes!"

"No! I'm not doing anything with your femininity and that's final!" He got off the couch and stomped to his bedroom.

Cass lay back into the leather cushions, smiling only when he slammed the door to make his point. So he walked away. He'd done it before. He always came back. It didn't matter if he wasn't there to help her at the moment. She already had a plan, a progressive way to prove to Luke—to everyone—that she wasn't someone to be pitied or dismissed.

Cassandra Bishop was going to become a girl.

"This isn't your night, Sel," Alice Panyon crowed to her husband a few hours later. She pulled in her third pot of the night with a smoky laugh.

"It's always my night, angel."

Cass smiled at the pair of them, the most improbable couple in all of Rancho Del Cielo. Where Selvyn Panyon was probably born in jeans and leather, Alice was the epitome of a debutante; cool, blonde and perfect. Ironically, Sel grew up to be a world-renowned artist while Alice was a retired firefighter. They were probably the happiest couple in town, too, with one little girl and another baby due to make an appearance sometime in the next few weeks. Not that a high, round belly kept Alice from stretching her arms around a pile of multicolored chips and chortling greedily.

Sel smoothed a wisp of Alice's white-blonde hair behind her ear, a gesture so intimate and familiar, Cass looked at the cards with a sense of guilt at having watched. Even jealousy. No one ever touched her like that.

But *someone* would.

Like a vow, the sentence ran through her mind as the cards ran through her fingers. When she did lift her eyes again, it wasn't to spy on Alice and Sel, or to see what May Belle and Jimmy were conspiring about this time, or even if Ben Friedly was trying to swipe another handful of popcorn from the bowl on the counter. It was to look at Burke as she shuttled cards around the table.

He hadn't made eye contact all evening but she concentrated on him until he couldn't avoid her any more. A deep blue, Burke's eyes were those of a man who thought, probably too much. He did everything deep in his head; math, bills, itinerary, designs for the cars he rebuilt from heaps. In the span of two minutes, the man could mentally take apart an entire engine and put it back together using all the pieces. Didn't take him much longer in real life either. His entire life was about plan of attack. If anyone should appreciate her setting a goal, it would be Burke. Normally.

Right now, she could tell he was thinking too much again. Chomping at the bit to get the evening's game over with so he could send her home with a pat on the head before having to discuss "the femininity plan". Well, she'd just have to get around that, now wouldn't she?

"Dealer's choice. Five-card stud, aces high, favor game. Showdown rules."

There were a few grumbles around the table, but no one complained about the game choice. Favor games were where you had to bet a favor instead of chips. Showdown rules meant in the case of only two players still holding, they could *request* a favor instead betting one. Burke eyed her suspiciously before reaching to the breakfast bar for the phone pad of paper and a pen. Cass gave him her best smile.

He almost knocked his chair over.

She stifled a laugh and set the leftover deck in front of herself. Carefully, she looked at her cards. Two queens, two aces and a deuce. She fought the urge to smile again as she lay down her deuce and slid it over to Jimmy. Burke was *so* going to lose.

They passed the pad around and by the time it made a full circle, the pot held a portrait sketch, a casserole, a lawn mowing, three free gallons of milk, a free dinner from Shaky Jakes and a Garth Brooks CD. Cass scowled. Damn, she better win this hand.

Right before she was about to call, Burke said he wanted to raise. He scribbled over the rights to his kitchen radio.

Fine, she could play dirty, too. She wrote her note and tossed it into the pot.

Jimmy leaned over and read her rotten handwriting by squinting one eye. "A date?"

"Gotta have one to take to Luke's wedding, don't I?"

She could have dropped a pin on the carpet and heard it snag.

Finally, Jimmy coughed. "Most of us here are married, CB. 'Cept Burke. You sure you wanna drag him to a wedding?" *In other words, are you sure you want to go to the wedding?*

"Pass me off to someone. You meet more people than I do, Jimmy. I'm sure Sel could find someone if it came down to it. Alice and May Belle keep trying to set me up with people, so there's no problem there."

Sel gave his wife a worried glance. Alice shrugged. What else was she supposed to do? It was true.

"What am I supposed to do with it?" Burke's baritone demanded.

Cass made herself shrug. "I don't know. Use it?"

His brows crashed together hard enough to clang.

"Give it to one of the guys at the shop. Pawn me off on a customer. Whatever you want."

"You're going to let us hand you off to some stranger?" Alice asked, each word enunciated with care, eyes darting from Cass to Burke and back. Cass nodded, waiting for the sign that Burke was paying attention.

There it was, the twitch of his eye when he thought she was doing something stupid. Reverse psychology was invented for Burke Halifax. No way would he let her go on a date with some stranger he didn't know. Even if he had to suffer himself.

Cass prepared herself for a hell of a game.

He should have throttled her while she was sleeping. Should have let her get pneumonia by sleeping on his front porch in the rain. He should have done anything but let her play poker tonight. The evil gleam in those green eyes warned she was about to be more trouble than she was worth but did he listen? No, of course not. That would have made sense. Now he was stuck watching the brat try to make him wriggle like a worm on a hook.

"Your bet, Jimmy." Cass blinked innocently at the older man on her left. *Ha! If she's innocent, I'm the mayor of Munchkinland.*

Jimmy slipped a glance over to Burke, who knew he didn't have to bother shaking his head. Jimmy ran the only grocery in town. He survived Korea, thirty-five years of marriage, two children, and most recently four years of marriage to May Belle. The man knew when to throw in the cards.

May watched her husband, shrugged and tossed down her five as well. "Sorry, CB, Burke looks about ready to bust a vein. If I set you up, we have to do it discreetly."

May Belle's main clientele were gamblers and gossips. If they did it, they'd be doing it over his dead body.

CB smiled, nodding her head like a queen. Of course. She was getting what she wanted.

Sel leaned forward to look around Alice's abundant stomach to check with Burke like Jimmy had before him. "I do know this one guy—"

"No, you don't, honey." Alice splayed her hand over Sel's cards and laid them on the table. Hers quickly followed suit. "And neither do I."

God, she better not be in on whatever CB was up to. Burke would hate to get angry with a pregnant woman.

He stared down at his own cards and wondered if he could beat her. They might only be fives, but it was hard to beat a three of a kind. He decided to risk it. All he had to do was take her bet and never call her on it. Easy as pie. "Call."

"You can't call."

"What? Why?"

"Showdown rules. It's just you and me now. I get to request a favor from you."

If she said even one damn word about finding her femininity, he was going to kill her and let the coroner look for it. Wrap both hands around that long neck of hers and squeeze till she popped. No one could convict him, either. Through gritting teeth he made himself ask, "Fine. What do you want?"

Cats with cream didn't look as pleased with themselves. She licked her lips, startling a rise out of him that had no business rising. You'd think his desire to do her in might have the smallest effect on him. At least his temper should have tamped the problem. It probably would have, but his worst nightmare began right before his eyes.

Cass leaned forward, wet lips pursed and pink, and said the words a man should never hear from his best friend. "It's simple, Burke. I want you to make me a woman."

Chapter Three

"You...want me to...*what?*"

Cass nodded her head along with each of his barely formed words. "Make me into a woman. You know, teach me how to dress, how to attract men. You said you could see my femininity. I want you to point it out and train it." She looked around the table from one slack-jawed face to another, before turning back to Burke's reddening countenance. "What did you think I meant?"

"Game's over, everyone." Burke put his cards down so slow Cass couldn't tell if he was mad or stunned.

Chairs moved in a flutter of activity. Sel helped Alice to her feet while Jimmy ushered a protesting May Belle toward the front door. It took all of ten seconds to end up alone in a room with him. Alone in the house. He stared at her, unblinking. Cass was pretty sure the verdict on his state of mind was mad.

Very mad.

"I said no," he reminded in a deadly soft voice. "I said it more times than I'd like to count or remember. You're fine the way you are, why can't you be happy with that?"

Cass stared down at her cards, willing herself not to crumple them in her fist. "Because I'm not."

"You were before the jackass came back to town. Why are you letting Luke decide what's important and what's not?"

She stood, angry at his blindness. How could he know her for so long, be present for every heartache, and think she had anything to be happy about? "Who told you I was happy? When was I *ever* happy with the way I am?"

His frown spread like a dark cloud across his brow. "You always seemed happy to me."

"Because you weren't looking." Or listening. Or paying any kind of attention, apparently. She crossed the length of the table and laid her cards in front of him. A full house, aces high. "No one has ever looked at me the way Sel looks at Alice. They just assume I would never want them to. Did you ever wonder how that makes me feel? To know no one will ever see me and think of me as anything more than an extension of the men in my life. All anyone sees is Hayne's sister, Burke's friend and Luke's pathetic cast-off. No one even uses my name anymore. I'm a pair of frickin' initials." She blinked back tears, stating facts he seemed dead-set on ignoring.

"Well, not anymore. Whether you help me or not, I'm going to the wedding and I'm going to prove to everyone, even you, that I'm more than a couple of letters. I'm a *woman*, damn it, and its time people finally figured it out. Especially me."

Burke said nothing while she stomped toward the front door, stopping briefly at the closet to pull out his jacket—the suede one he almost never wore, thank you very much—and shrug it on. His Neanderthal brow lowered and she was almost sure she heard him growl, but he still didn't say anything. Angrier now than she could remember being since Luke came home, she yanked open his front door, ready to bum a ride from any of the people still waiting outside to see what happened. But before she went, she wanted to make sure he had something to truly stew over.

"Oh and Burke? In case you missed it, dumb ass, you lost the game."

♥ ♥ ♥

"Didn't work, did it?" May Belle slid a plate with a half-pound mushroom and guacamole burger and steak fries across the glossy table to Cass.

She reached for the burger, dejected. "Nope."

"Hon, if you wanted a make-over, you could have come to me. You don't need Burke for it."

"He's the only person who seemed to think I had what it takes to be a girl." She still smarted at his dismissal. Somewhere in the back of her mind, she suspected he was trying to bluff his way out of a lie, but if she had any hope of changing her future as the Spinster-Time-Forgot, she had to believe him. Or convince him to believe it. Neither one seemed all too possible.

May Belle made a snorting sound resembling laughter. "Hon, trust me, if you need a bra, you got what it takes."

Cass looked down.

May shrugged as she reconsidered. "Well, if a supermodel can do without, so can you."

"Thanks, May. I feel much better now."

"Hey, they aren't bad. It's kinda hard to tell what you got under such a big T-shirt."

"It's a work shirt." Cass plucked at the collar of the dark green polo. She stole it from Hayne ages ago. Was it a boosters shirt from one of his sports? Maybe he got it for a school event—

"It's a rag." May Belle settled into the bench seat on the opposite side of the booth, jarring Cass from her unimportant mental rambling. May tapped the table with her manicured nail, red lips curled at one corner. "Are you serious about going to Luke's wedding or were you just trying to get Burke's goat?"

Cass pushed her plate to the side.

May Belle's penciled brows rose in surprise. "You *are* serious."

She laughed. "Burke's got very small goats. Not a lot of challenge there."

The older woman nodded. Few things were as well documented as Burke's incapacity for change. "You know he's not going to like this, right?"

"Burke or Luke?" Cass felt her grin start to form at the left corner of her mouth. The right side caught up, leaving her smiling like an idiot. Hate would be a better word, in either case.

"Doesn't look like it matters. How much time do we have ?"

"Two weeks." Fifteen days, to be precise.

"Speedy little sucker, ain't he?" May tsked.

"Not where I was concerned."

May Belle ceased clicking her tongue to eye Cass again. "You sure you're doing this for the right reasons, honey? I'd hate for you to expect this to change anything between you and Luke."

Cass had to shake her head. Someday, people might realize she wasn't hung up on Luke Hansen the way they all seemed to think. If she pulled this off, that day might be sooner than anyone could have expected. "I hope it does, I truly do. But don't worry, May, I don't want Luke back. I'm thinking of this thing as finally washing that man out of my life."

"If that's how you feel, free this afternoon?" May pulled her ordering pad from her apron and started scribbling a list. Cass watched a flurry of words form under the pencil.

"I guess I could—"

"Good. I want you to meet me in an hour at Lola's."

Lola Velasquez was Rancho Del Cielo's sole beauty parlor owner. She had three girls there to do manicures, pedicures and styling, but most people went to see her. She was fifty or sixty—no one knew for sure—but nothing stopped her from wearing three-inch heels, perfect make-up or revolving shades of hair color. Her chair was also rumored to have the sanctity of a confessional, which caused droves of women to schedule for romantic advice alone. Cass never needed Lola's talents in either situation.

Until now.

"Lola's, an hour."

"And honey?"

Cass looked up from the plate she was sliding toward herself.

May Belle gestured to it. "No more of those."

Cass stared down in surprise. The sesame-bunned, double-pattied, half-pound burger weeping tomato juice and guacamole onto her fingers stared back. With longing. "Why?"

"First rule of being a woman is dieting."

"But I don't need a diet!" Hell, she had to eat all the time as it was just to keep up with what she burned on the job.

"Neither do most other women. From now on it's salads and water. No more eating like a man."

That stung. "I *work* like a man."

"Second rule of being a woman: work harder than men so you can be even with them, and do it with less than them."

Starve and work harder. That didn't sound like femininity. It sounded like torture. "How many of these so-called rules are there?"

May Belle slid out of the booth and headed back toward the bar. "You better buy a notebook. See you in an hour!"

"That was just mean!"

"It was wax, *chulita*, and trust me, it's better."

"It hurt like hell!"

"Beauty hurts." It had to be the tenth time Lola got to say that and smile. Cass was ready to rip out Lola's dark burgundy hair and she'd only been there for two hours. So far, her eyebrows were waxed, her hands soaked for her manicure as were her feet. Unfortunately, they were long done with those pleasantries. Lola pulled off only one of the long, wax-covered strips from Cass's left leg. There were plenty left to yank. Not to mention a whole other leg.

"You scream a lot for someone everybody calls tough."

Cass said something singeing.

Lola laughed…and tore another strip.

For fifty minutes, the pattern repeated until Cass was allowed to stumble out of the waxing room and over to the styling chair. Her only consolation was that she'd been able to talk Lola out of a bikini wax. Once she'd discovered what it was.

"Now, we do your hair. What color do you want? Blonde, like May Belle said? Men go crazy for *la rubias*. I know, I was one once." Her raspy little giggle had enough dirty in it to make Cass smile despite the stinging skin. Lola pushed Cass's chair into to a prone position.

May Belle must have talked a lot in the hour before Cass arrived. Lola had emptied her entire day, armed with a suggestion from the former beauty queen on every single topic. May Belle herself was gone only God knew where, leaving Cass at the mercy of the Hispanic whirlwind with a whisking brush.

Warm water sprayed onto her scalp and Lola's hands began massaging. Cass closed her eyes in heavenly bliss. This was the first thing that felt good. But as she closed her eyes and tried to envision herself as a cool blonde, all she could see was Sally. Tiny, perfect Sally. Whatever enjoyment she had soured.

"No. Luke would expect me to try copying his cute little Pomeranian. No, no blonde."

Lola was quiet for a while, scrubbing, massaging and rinsing. "*Mira*, you have a lot of red in here. *Ay, por qué no pensé antes?* Let's make it all red. It'll look good with your coloring, no? Those eyes, *tambien*. I'll trim it, you'll look exactly like Rita Hayworth."

Cass seriously doubted it, but since she didn't have a clue who Rita Hayworth *was* she kept her thoughts to herself. Lola rambled on about bone structure and eye color and a whole bunch of things that didn't make much sense.

"You look like your mother," She interjected out of nowhere, humming as she sudsed. "She had the prettiest hair."

Cass stared up at her, shocked. "You knew my mother?"

Lola nodded, not looking away from her work. "*Claro*. She was one of my best friends, but everyone felt that way about her. When she died, the whole town came for her funeral. Everyone wanted to be like her and your daddy. He never saw anyone but her. He still doesn't." Lola's expression flickered with disappointment before she pasted a blinding smile on her face. "*Y por qué no?* She was beautiful. Kind. Everybody loved Lora."

Cass knew all that. She was too young when Lora's lung cancer took hold, so all her impressions of her mother came from photographs and her father's occasional remarks. She had a hard time believing Eddie was ever the life of any party, but according to the older folks, he and Lora were once the fairy tale of the town. Lora's death remained its greatest tragedy. Had Lola been trying to get Eddie's attention or something? Poor woman, nuclear weapons couldn't get Eddie's attention these days.

"You don't remember her, do you?" Lola asked, something soothing in her quiet tone.

Cass shook her head. "Just her pictures. And her smile." Her memories were almost entirely sensory, more what she thought of instead of actual events. A scent of lilac and sunshine, a soft hand in

hers…a smile. Something about Lora's cheeky grin made Cass think
her mother had a wild streak a mile wide. Thinking of that smile gave
her comfort whenever she got in trouble for misbehaving. It would be
nice to think she got more than red hair from her mother.

"Hmm, *qué lastima.* You would have liked her, *chulita.* She grew the
most beautiful roses. She could make any plant grow, just the way she
touched it. She had that way. Like you." Lola abruptly pushed the seat
into an upright position.

Cass grabbed the armrests to stay on. "My father says the same
thing." *When he talks.*

"How is your daddy?"

Cass squinted an eye at the mirror. *She is interested!*

Lola was hardly flustered, but the towel she was using to dry
Cass's hair was moving a little more vigorously than before. "Back
when I first moved here from Chula Vista with my husband, he and
your mama made sure everyone knew about my shop. It wasn't so easy
for a Mexican to run her own business in those days. They helped a
lot. My Danny used to drive trucks. When he was gone, Lora asked
your daddy to come check on us, make sure everything was okay until
Danny came back. We thought it was sweet how he opened the
nursery for Lora. Romantic."

Cass laughed. She'd never thought of the nursery as particularly
romantic, but since they still sold Lora's breed of roses, she had to
admit Lola was probably on to something.

"I never see Eddie any more. Not since my Danny passed away."
She paused in her brush selection to bless herself with the sign of the
cross.

"He doesn't get out much these days." *Understatement of the decade.*

"Well, you tell him I asked about him."

Cass raised an eyebrow in the mirror.

Lola winked back. "*Pero,* we're here for you, today. What do you say, we go red, no?"

Cass ignored the shiver of excitement and terror coursing through her. The time had come. Everything she'd done so far had been simple and mostly unnoticeable. Shoot, most of it would grow out in a few days. This would be the first drastic change, the first step to bigger and better things. It was perfectly fine to be nervous. She shuddered a breath, closed her eyes and took the plunge. "We go red."

Burke walked into Shaky Jakes with a sense of dread. It wouldn't go away. All day it hung on like a bad smell. Something in the world had gone horribly, terribly wrong. He just didn't know what.

He'd tried to track CB, to make sure she hadn't gone and broken something vital, but hadn't been able to reach her anywhere. Hayne complained about her taking the afternoon off, making his unease stronger. Figuring she was here for dinner, Burke wandered into the crowd.

The number of people wasn't disconcerting. There was always a crowd at Shaky Jakes. Several of them even looked familiar, former A-crowd cronies from high school. He hadn't liked them then and usually groaned when he had to deal with them now. But there were a number of faces there he didn't know. In a town the size of Rancho Del Cielo, it was another cause for alarm. A fast scan of the place didn't silence the bells ringing in his head. The only woman by herself was a redhead at the bar with Ben Friedly, of all people. Burke gave her a passing glance, though the rippling auburn hair did stop him for a second. So did the soft cotton dress hugging her body. She had a 40's flashback look to her, especially with those seamed stockings leading to sturdy black heels on the bar rail. Great legs, but not CB.

Ten minutes later, he'd checked every booth and was back at the front door without sign of her. The party was getting rowdy and Burke noticed a number of men were pointing at the redhead. Despite being about to leave, he decided to give her another look over. The men didn't appear all that complimentary.

He couldn't figure out why. She had her back to him, but her curves all seemed to be in the right place. The hair was a real bonus, the kind of rich color that made him ache to touch it. The dress was one of those short sleeve numbers, leaving long lengths of browned arms showing. Odd, a redhead browning so nicely. His eyes combed over her slim ribcage, down the length of her spine to a pair of sweetly curving hips and—

If a man felt his heart stop and his breath still, wasn't he was dead?

The entire bar rattled to a stop for some reason. All heads turned his way, all except for the redhead. But, she wouldn't, of course; the hiding, sneaking, disguised little brat.

Burke finally realized why everyone was staring at him. He'd bellowed her name with all the rising frustration in him. Unfortunately for her, there was more on the way.

"If you know what's good for you, you'll turn around, CB."

Her head shook violently.

"Goddamn it, don't make me come over there!"

"Go away!"

It was her all right. She sounded like she had a cold or something. There was some snickering from the crowd of men, all of which made Burke tone it down a degree. No point dragging the whole town into it, even if it was a bit late. He stomped over to her stool and tugged on her shoulder to spin her stool around. It didn't do much good. CB had her face buried in a towel full of ice.

"What the hell happened to you?" He tried to pull on the pack, but she was determined to keep it there. Aside from decking her, there was no way to loosen her grip. He turned to Ben on the corner stool.

The old man shook his head at him, his rheumy, drooping eyes filled with disdain. "Boy, you have all the sensitivity of a bull moose."

From the top of his spiky white hair, past his sun-darkened leathery skin and sloping shoulders to his gnarled, arthritic hands, Ben Friedly was about as sensitive as the Boogie Man. "Coming from you, that could be a compliment."

"Could be, but it ain't. She was fine not ten minutes ago, but…she…uh, got some red things on her face."

"Red things?"

"Yeah, red things. Welts or something. May said she was prob'ly allergic to the foundation, but don't ask me. I ain't never seen her get sick from the foundation in this place before." Ben shrugged and reached for a bowl of pretzels. "Before that, those guys were over here knocking each other out trying to get her to dance with them. But when those blister things started showing up…Well, outsiders never did have any class." Ben patted CB's knee paternally. "May went to get something for her, but she's been gone forever."

Burke had an unsettling feeling in his stomach. It felt like guilt, but he wasn't in a rush to name it. Instead, he tapped on the icepack. "Cassie? Honey, let me see. Maybe I can help."

"No, you can't. You know less about make-up than me."

"Paint's paint, Cassie."

She said something very CB.

Burke smiled. If she could call him names, she couldn't be that bad. "Come on, let me take a look."

"You say one mean thing to me, Burke Halifax, and I swear you'll never have children."

"Yeah, yeah, put down the towel." He waited for another few seconds until she dropped her hands. "Ugh!"

The ice popped back up and she was calling him worse names than usual. There was a roar of laughter from the men in the crowd at the other side of the bar.

"Cassie, I'm sorry, hon, you…surprised me is all." *More like scared the crap out of me, but why bring up semantics?* "You have to give a guy some warning."

"It's that bad?"

Burke scratched the back of his head. Truth be told, it was. Dozens of oozing, blistery welts dotted her face from forehead to chin. Even her eyelids and her lips. With all the smeared colors, she looked like lumpy ice cream in the sun.

"Let me look again." He didn't want to look, though. In fact, he'd feel better never to see that again, but she was embarrassed and way the hell over her head. He was her best bet until May Belle came back. *Come on, May…* "I promise not to say anything if it doesn't help."

CB shrugged and lowered the ice, slowly this time. The welts were still there and a good number more than he realized. As she dragged the towel down, she took the worst of the make-up with it, leaving color smears, yes, but at least her features were still where they were supposed to be.

Burke breathed a sigh of relief. "Oh, this isn't bad. What we need is a way to get it off. Who put this crap on you anyway?"

"May Belle."

Which meant it was piled on like street pavement. "Your skin probably couldn't breathe."

"It's itchy," she mewled through puffy lips.

"Well, don't scratch." Burke picked up the icepack and freed a corner to wipe more of the inky eyeliner off her cheek. Lipstick came next. It reminded him of when she was four or so and Hayne used to wipe her face after dinner. She'd sit like an obedient doll, the only time she stayed still at that age. At any age, really.

Before long, her lips were a rosy pink again, if reddened in a few spots. It was odd, having her stare up at him while he dabbed and wiped. Almost intimate. Suddenly, he was looking down and seeing her face, as if he'd never looked at it before.

Hell if she wasn't pretty, even with all those bumps. Her eyes glowed, a little greener than he remembered, her cheekbones looked smooth and soft beneath his fingertips. Had she always had such a fragile jawbone, the stubborn chin jutting out until it was almost cute? He didn't remember her that way, but it was undoubtedly CB there. Just...more.

She curled her fingers around his wrist when he ran out of things to clean but hadn't found a reason to remove his hands yet. "Burke—"

The crowd of men roared again at the sound of the front door's bells, making them both blink. Burke stepped back, handing her the towel and mentally shoving at the flush of heat that had no explanation. CB was pink again, but he wasn't about to clean any more make-up off her. Ever. Unfortunately, he turned to see what was making Ben cackle like mad, finding only the old man's bushy eyebrows waggling back at him.

"Hey, Halifax! Who's the filly?"

Burke whirled to see Luke Hanson standing on the threshold of Shaky Jakes. He finally understood who the strangers mixed with the locals in the bar were. Luke's friends—mostly old, some new. It was some sort of impromptu party for the schmuck, and of course, CB had to go waltzing right into it. The girl had the luck of a troll.

As he was about to tell Luke to do something unpleasant to himself, CB reached out and grabbed his arm again. Luckily, her back was still to Luke, but of course she recognized his voice. She shook her head in a staccato motion, a look as close to begging as she could get in her eyes. Didn't she know he couldn't take it when she looked like that?

"No one you'd know, Hanson."

Her grateful expression was going to do him in one of these days. He hated how she cared in the slightest what a jerk like Luke thought of her. He especially hated that she cared so much she'd do all this to herself. He reached out and brushed a wet tendril of rich red behind her ear, earning himself a sheen of tears and more damn gratitude. The bitterness in his mouth was getting hard to smile through.

Someday, she'd forget Luke. She'd go back to liking who she was. But until then, he figured he should keep her from making a fool of herself over the bastard.

"We have to get you out of here," he whispered in her ear.

She nodded, allowing him to turn her in the stool to keep her back to Luke's curious stare. "One big problem."

"What's that?"

"I can't walk in these heels. I barely made it to the stool last time."

"You always have to make things more difficult than they already are, don't you?" He sighed while she laid her forehead against his chest, rubbing her face against the fabric of his cotton shirt. Momentarily distracted by the odd feeling, it took him a few seconds to see she wasn't affectionately nuzzling him. "I said no scratching."

Her head stopped moving.

"You gave me an idea though. Maybe we can get you out without his recognizing you if you pretend to be drunk. Think you can make it believable?"

"Sure, I'm probably still drunk from the other night anyway."

"Whatever works." He bent down to take the shoes off her feet. Did she always have such small ankles? Must be the nylons. CB was the sturdiest woman he knew. Shoes in hand, he righted himself, slipped an arm around her waist and tucked her head under his chin. With any luck, Luke would be too tied up with his friends to notice them. Only five more feet to the door…

"Getting them liquored up first these days, Halifax?"

Burke could see the front door close enough to touch, but Luke's voice sounded closer. Resigned, he half-turned and found Luke right behind him, already holding a beer by the neck. His eyes had faint bruises beneath them and his nose was swollen and discolored with a small band-aid across the bridge. All in all, CB had nailed him a good one. Unfortunately, she hadn't gotten him in the mouth so the punk could still smirk.

"Go back to your friends," Burke warned. "They came a long way to see you."

"They'll still be there in a few minutes. Unless you wanna get this one out of her panties before she passes out." Only Luke could make that sound like an acceptable expectation.

"She's a friend, Hanson. I'm getting her home safe."

Luke grinned. "Sure."

Burke shrugged him off and started steering CB towards the door but Luke extended his beer hand to stop them. "I saw CB at your place this morning. When did she move in with you?"

"She didn't—" Burke flinched at the pinch to the inside of his underarm, "—mention seeing you."

Luke looked disappointed for a second, then took a swig of his beer. "Well, I guess she wouldn't. How long after I left did you two get together?"

"Who said we got together?" He ignored the prodding, giving her an extra squeeze to push the air out of her.

Luke eyed him curiously, tipping his head to the side in dismissal. "It wouldn't take a rocket scientist to figure it out. She answers your door in your clothes after a shower, it's kinda obvious."

As if the obvious were really Luke's forte.

"Isn't it a little ironic, my finding you doing exactly what you busted my chops over last year."

CB straightened and it was all Burke could do to keep her bent over in a semi-prone position.

"Guess you're human after all, eh, Hallifax?" Luke laughed as he brought the beer up to his lips. "Even *you* couldn't live with CB forever."

Burke almost forgot to hold her down at the pithy remark. "You aren't going to overstretch your intelligence to compare us, are you?"

"*Us?* Nah, why bother? The only thing we have in common is CB." Luke seemed to remember his assumption that Burke was seeing her because he smiled. "But hey, if you like your women flat as pancakes, she's the one for you. Me, I like 'em curvy and curvier."

Cass's blunt nails clawed into Burke's arm in an effort to escape. He moved his foot to cover her bare toes and pushed down until she made a muffled sound into his shirt and gave up.

"Funny, last I heard you liked them butch and butchier."

Luke soured immediately. "You know better than anyone that rumor isn't true."

"Do I? I read the letter where you wrote it yourself."

Luke stood straighter, darting his eyes to his friends before facing Burke again, his voice low and angry. "No one else was supposed to have read it, asshole."

How lame could one guy get? "You were with her for over ten years, moron. People were going to want to know why you left her. You should have come up with a smarter lie if you didn't want her to believe it. What *I* find ironic is how no one here seemed real surprised. Not one of those women you were always catting around with, not one of your so-called friends. In fact, everyone believed it hook, line and sinker."

Luke scowled. It didn't last long, must've hurt. The wuss. "You think I care what this Podunk town thinks of me?"

"So why bother getting married here? Everyone is nice and happy as things are." *Lord knows I was.*

"Well, I'm not. That b—" He cut himself off abruptly when Burke lurched his way. Luke might have been dumb enough to stand there and take it when Cass lit into him, but they both knew he'd need his head surgically removed from his ass if Burke took to beating on him. "She broke my nose! Humiliated me in front of my fiancée."

Burke shrugged. "You humiliated her in front of a whole town for years. I'd say it's fair."

"Well, it's *not* fair. It's not gonna be until everyone knows the truth."

Maybe ass-surgery would be needed after all. It'd be a kind of a lobotomy. Mindful of the bundle of Cass in his arms, Burke lowered his voice so—hopefully—only Luke would hear. "The real truth or the edited-for-television kind? Neither one paints you as the good guy, pretty boy."

Luke's eyes narrowed, but he didn't reply.

"Yeah, that's what I thought." Burke backed away, shaking his head. At least this mess would be over now. "Do yourself a favor, stay the hell away from CB and take your grandstand of a wedding with you." He moved toward the door, pulling CB's too quiet and too obedient body with him.

"What goes on between me and CB has nothing to do with you, Halifax," Luke sputtered, making Burke stop once more.

A glance over his shoulder showed more of Luke's city friends had moved in to see what the deal was. That explained the sudden tiny pair of balls. *Perfect. Just perfect.*

"You were always right there in our business, like some kinda watch dog," Luke rattled on. "I didn't like it much then and I sure as hell don't like it now."

"You wanna do something about it?" *Don't I wish?* Luke Hanson might be pretty and even popular, but the likelihood of his taking the challenge—even with his friends around him—was right up there with Burke putting on a dress and doing the tango with Humphrey Bogart.

"What's the point? CB's nothing to me anymore. She wasn't much to me when we were dating." Luke shrugged, gesturing over his shoulder for his friends to see and pay closer attention. Like lemmings, they quieted to follow his cue. "I'm gonna marry Sally; show everyone in this town that I'm not what they think I am. Truth is, CB Bishop was lucky to ever have me."

Burke wasn't sure when it happened, but CB's pretense of clinging to him had become real, her clench tight enough to hurt. What made it worse was that he had the feeling Luke wouldn't have said a word different if he knew she was there. Maybe he'd said it to her all before. It would certainly explain her sudden lack of confidence. In an instant, he hated the bastard even more.

"Is that why you invited her to your wedding? To make sure she saw you marrying the better woman?" Burke asked, loud enough to silence the crowded bar. People leaned out of their booths, some concerned, most interested. Ben Friedly watched, his wrinkled face not expressing an opinion one way or the other.

Luke had one. His eyes glinted pride. "Damn straight."

"You've never been a smart man, Hanson. Most have said damn stupid. You never deserved CB. You couldn't tell what a good woman you had, not even when she was haulin' your ass out of trouble time and again. So I'm going to put this in terms even a fool like you can understand. I'll bet that at your wedding, when CB walks into the church, everyone in this town will be calling you an idiot for giving up the best thing you ever had."

Nails bit into his waist but Burke wasn't about to stop now. For once it seemed so clear. The way to show CB what a slime her ex was and if anything was ever wrong, it was that she was too good for Luke in the first place.

Luke laughed loudly, extending his arms wide. "The mighty Burke Halifax is gonna make a bet with *me*? In front of everybody?" The bar remained quiet, waiting for his response. No one ever said Luke wasn't a showman. He nodded his curly blond head in a mock salute. Hell if the entire place didn't exhale at the same time. "Sure, why not?" He laughed, yukking it up for the crowd. "It's not like I can lose."

"Name your price." Now that he'd started this thing, Burke wanted it over in a hurry.

"You know what I want." For the first time ever, Luke Hanson looked dangerous. The rat bastard.

Since pride was at stake—especially since it wasn't even his own pride—Burke couldn't back down. Not even if he wanted to. Maybe it was temper. Maybe it was simply past time someone dealt with Luke out in the open, but Burke found himself agreeing despite the nudging and gripping at his waist. "Fine. I'll bet you the Z-28 that when she comes to that wedding she'll be the finest looking—"

"And acting!" Luke interjected, setting Burke's teeth to gritting. "She has to be a real lady or it don't mean diddly. Slapping some stripes on an old car don't make it fast."

Burke felt like slapping something all right. "—and *acting*, lady there."

Luke laughed, inspiring his buddies to join in, even though not a single one of them seemed to have a clue what the joke was. "Not that it'll matter, but what happens if you pull this miracle off?"

"You stay out of my town. But before you go, you apologize to CB for using her, hurting her and being the most pitiful excuse for dog crap ever spawned. There at the wedding, on bended knee, until she accepts your apology."

Luke considered it. "That's it? No cash?"

Burke worked not to roll his eyes. It wasn't any fun using veiled insults on the clinically moronic. "Why bother?" he asked, mimicking Luke. "My reward will be watching you grovel." He offered his hand, letting CB stand on her own.

Luke grinned as if someone had given him the winning lottery ticket. He slid his hand into Burke's and shook for all he was worth. "Hell, this is gonna be more fun than I thought."

Yeah. Burke grimaced as reality took a nibble out of his grim satisfaction, *fun.*

Chapter Four

For someone who'd gotten her way, CB sure threw a big snit. Of the two of them, Burke figured as he drove them to his house, *he* was the one who should have an attitude. He was the one doing the last thing on earth he should be, but there she was, scrunching herself as close to the door as she could, practically on her side and facing away from him. A furtive glance her way gave him one more reason to be upset.

Her position gave him an excellent view of her backside.

Burke rubbed his face with a tired hand. It was bad enough that eyeing her butt was the only way he'd recognized her in the bar, he didn't have to have it facing him and taunting him because it was on the wrong woman. He gripped the steering wheel until he heard the leather creak beneath his palms.

"I'm sorry I bet your car, okay?" He wasn't, but if she didn't turn over he wasn't going to be responsible for his actions. His thoughts were already in bad places.

She said nothing.

Okay, not mad about the car. She was mad about something else. It didn't take deep thought to figure out what it was.

"I'm sorry you had to find out this way."

She turned her head toward him a little bit. More toward the windshield, but he'd take what he could get. "About what?"

He swallowed the guilt that tried to lodge in his throat. "About Luke."

She leaned forward more, her skin squeaking on the glass.

"Cheating on you," he added, well aware there were a few other things she may have put together on her own to worry about.

She turned back to the side window, making another squeak. "Oh...that."

"You want to talk about it?"

"Do you hear me talking about it?"

"You should, you know. It'll help."

"How would *you* know?"

Good question. No woman had ever cheated on him. Of course, he was never committed to a woman long enough for her to cheat on him. He dated and he'd had girlfriends for a few weeks, but no one lasted long. It was the thing CB ribbed him about most.

All his friends had long since moved away or married. Even Sel, the one no one thought would settle down, had a wife and family. Of course, Sel claimed the only woman he ever wanted was Alice. Burke didn't have such a convenient cop out. He realized long ago he wasn't made like everyone else. Love came easy to some people. For Cass, love came hard. For him, it never came at all. "It's what I've heard."

"Been watching Oprah again?"

"No, I have not, thank you very much." Not this week, anyway. It wasn't his fault. His shift manager, Rafael, was hooked on the show. He claimed his wife insisted they watch it so they could have something to talk about at home, but the truth was Rafael liked it. Burke allowed it because 'Fael's wife bought the television and installed it herself. Unfortunately, the only place quiet enough to watch it was in his office. It made the paperwork go a little faster, if only to escape.

"Luke's cheating doesn't matter."

Well, that was heartening. "Good. It was a long time ago anyway."

She went back to being silent, turned away from him, her hip curving upward only a few inches from the stick shift he gripped like a lifeline. The second he had to go into reverse he was going to be rubbing his hand against the Promised Land. He bit off a groan, too damn aware of every shadow and curve of her ass. It took work to keep his eyes on the road, especially when she bounced slowly in the seat, forward to the glass, backward toward his hand. If she shifted another inch he'd be feeling it even sooner. He fought the urge to tap his foot because he didn't want to turn a simple drive home into a carnival ride. With two minutes left until they got to his house, he couldn't take it anymore.

"Will you please sit up?"

"Why?"

"Because you look like the puppy left in the pet store. Why the hell are you rocking like that?"

"The glass is cool. I'm rubbing the bumps."

If she didn't quit, he'd be rubbing something too, dammit. "Stop acting like a spoiled brat and sit up."

"No."

"No?"

"Leave me alone and drive, Burke."

Great. She did care about Hanson's cheating. At least her problem drenched his over-eager libido in cold water. "Cassie, Luke isn't worth sulking over. If the conversation back there didn't prove that to you, I don't know what will."

"All I picked up was that there was something going on between you and Luke I didn't know about before." She finally shifted at the red light, sitting up and crossing her arms under her breasts. Sweet God, where was her bra? The criss-crossing flaps forming the top of her dress flopped open, showing enough curved mounds to make his throat constrict. He could see the whole of her sternum; right down to the little mole he used to tickle when she was six years old. A horn honked, reminding him time didn't stop for everyone.

Cass raised her eyebrows and he gunned the engine. It should have been easy not to look at her, he was driving for Pete's sake, but she didn't seem to notice the loose dress and he couldn't mention it. Or stop sneaking glances at it.

"Hello? You going to fill me in or not?"

Not. He might want to, thoroughly and no holds barred, but filling her was not an option.

"Burke?"

Though there were only the passing streetlights to intermittently shine over her, he wondered if he were better off staring at the curve of her ass. Anything had to be better than trying to decide if he was seeing shadow or nipple.

"Burke!"

"What?"

"What was Luke talking about?"

The view—and the conversation—was definitely safer.

"What aren't you telling me?"

He snorted. "The possible answers are endless." And he'd tell her every single one of those possibilities before he coughed up the truth she wanted.

"About you and Luke," she clarified.

"Don't say our names like that. Makes us sound like a couple or something." He shuddered. In this town, one couldn't be too careful.

"Aren't you?" *Return of the snit.* Which was a good thing. The more she annoyed him, the less she'd arouse him. He hoped.

"Sorry, kid, the only one of us dumb enough to date Luke Hanson was you."

"So why are you lying for him?"

I'm lying for you. But he couldn't say that, no matter how hurt she sounded.

"What did you have to do with Luke leaving RDC?"

"Nothing." He wasn't stupid enough to think she'd let him get away without details. "I held the door open and the weasel ran through."

"What did you *do*, Burke?"

Nothing you'll ever find out about. "We talked. I said if he wasn't ready to marry you, he should go."

"Why did he say you knew he wasn't gay?"

Damn, that part always made him smile but CB wasn't in the mood to see him happy. "I have no idea."

"Why don't I believe you?"

He grinned despite her anger. Anger he could deal with. "Because you're an untrusting soul?"

She expelled her breath with an irritated noise. "You're as annoying as Luke. The both of you act like I need you to do my thinking."

"Hey, at least I never talk to you or about you the way he does."

"No, you talk *for* me like I'm a non-entity incapable of making rational decisions for myself." Now *she's mad about the car.* "I can't believe you bet my Z!"

"It's the only bet he would take and you know it." Luke's passion for CB's car was a thing of legend. First he'd begrudged her the time she spent with Burke putting it together. He broke up with her over it and she hadn't cared much, surprising the hell out of Burke and the town. Once the car was running, newly painted and roaring like a mountain lion, Luke came calling again. As usual, Cass took him back, but she never let him drive it. It stayed a sticking point between them that even the best of the local bookies couldn't give odds on.

Blessedly, she stayed quiet until he pulled up in front of his house.

"Do you really think we can pull this off?" she asked finally, the twinge of worry in her voice threatening to become full on pangs and twangs.

"Sure we can." *Or we'll die trying.* "You're a good person under all those bad habits. All we have to do is dig you out and shape you up."

"Great!" she complained, smacking her leg with loud frustration. "Even *you* do it!"

Burke frowned. "Do what?"

"Call me a person. It's annoying."

She was off her nut. There wasn't any other thing to call it. "Since when was being a good person a bad thing?"

"Since it means you don't see a woman. I'm a *woman*. In most cultures I'm an old maid."

"Twenty-eight isn't—"

"It's *old*. Do you realize my ovaries are—"

He almost covered his ears, but instead he cut the engine and opened his door. "I don't want to hear about your ovaries, CB. We'll figure a way to save the car, I swear, but mention your ovaries again and you're on your own."

"Well, at least you admit I have some," she grumbled.

When she made no move to get out, he shrugged. "Fine, you have some. Is this conversation done, I'm hungry."

"Why didn't you drop me off at home?"

Perfect, now she was suspicious. "Because we've only got two weeks to make *you* into a lady. In my book, that isn't a lot of time and in this situation…"

Even in the dark he could see her eyes narrow on him. "In this situation, what?"

Maybe it was time to admit they were both in over their heads. "In this situation, we're going to need all the time we can get."

♥ ♥ ♥

"You want me to *what?*" Cass knew she heard him, but she had to be wrong.

"Undo it. All of it. Put yourself back the way you were. The hair, the dress, the shoes. Whatever you did with May Belle, make it stop." He paced his living room, blue work shirt wrinkled, hair standing on end. If he kept this up, someone might think he was the one who'd spent the afternoon in a torture chamber.

"Do you know what I had to go through to get like this? I've had hair ripped out, Burke. From everywhere! I've been plucked, waxed, soaked, painted, teased, dried and bleached. I'm not doing it in reverse!"

He waved his hand, dismissing her agony with a wiggle of his blunt fingers. "You aren't a redhead, CB."

"Yes, I am." *Sorta.* "The hair stays." She crossed her arms and set her feet apart so he'd know she meant business.

"The only way I'm going to help you is if you do things my way. This isn't my way. This is—" His gaze spanned her from the top of her head to the tips of her toes, intense enough to start a weird tingly feeling where ever it touched. "I don't know that the hell that is but it's wrong."

The tingly feeling died. She rolled her eyes. *The control freak and his issues.* "I'm not dyeing it back. I can't anyway. It'll fry up and frizz or something if I do it too soon. Work with the red."

He made a noise she likened to growling. Half-grunt, half-grumble, all Burke. "Why are you always making everything difficult?"

Why does he always ask that? "I'm not betting cars, am I? You're the one who put us both on the line."

"You think I don't know that?" He looked like a bear with a sore paw, walking his living room as if it were a cage. "Stop it, you're standing like a man."

Cass dropped her arms in shock. Okay, it's true she'd never seen any of the ladies in town stand as if they were preparing to imitate the rock of Gibraltar. None of them argued with Burke Halifax on a regular basis, either. Come to think of it, Burke was the *reason* she stood like this. He was the one who taught her all those boxing techniques. In fact, if it weren't for him, she wouldn't be in this mess at all!

"Why are you looking at me like that?" he snapped.

"Because I'm wondering if you're the best person to help me." Alice might be a better bet. She oozed class and poise. But she had a daughter and a man eating up all her time. Kids Cass couldn't complain about. They were innocent and genuinely needed their mothers, but men? They devoured time like they did steaks—whole and often. No, she couldn't ask Alice to clear her schedule for two weeks at the drop of a hat.

Burke's eyes widened, relief slowing his feet and lifting the Cro-Magnon scowl. "Really?"

May Belle had already done all she could, Cass admitted while sneaking a scratch to her cheek. Lola's practices tended to leave one in pain. Hayne, usually so helpful when a girl needed a hand, wouldn't touch this project to save his life. If she could do it alone—could hope to find and shape some indefinable, untouchable thing inside herself— she would. But she couldn't. Galling or not, she needed help. Which left Burke. But she wasn't going to get much done until he admitted she would actually need to change something about herself if they were going to keep her car or her dignity.

If she didn't know him from his boots to his cowlick, that might be a daunting prospect.

She nodded, still pretending she had other options. "You're lousy at this."

Nothing got to Burke like implied failure. "Lousy?"

"Rotten lousy," she confirmed, trampling his need to be the best at everything he did. "You have no intention to make a girl out of me, Burke. You've spent most of your life making a *boy* out of me. My Dad and Hayne, I can understand; it was easier for them if I wasn't expecting frills and lace. But you seem to like me the way I've been."

Confusion filled his eyes. Poor guy. He truly didn't get it. "Of course I did. You're fine that way."

"The whole point of this stupid bet is to be completely different than I was. Until you get your head out of your ass and see that, you're no good to me." Shrugging as if it didn't matter—and it really, really did—she walked past him to the front door. She plucked his keys out of the crystal dish in the bookcase nearby.

"Where do you think you're going with those?"

"Home. You left my car back at Shaky Jakes. Again." She opened the door but, being Burke and it being his Explorer, he moved faster. The door clanged shut, his hand as flat against it as the line of his mouth.

"You can't go home in that getup."

She scoffed, plucking at the loose cotton. "I think Hayne and Dad will survive."

"Well, you're not driving my car."

"Fine. I'll walk in this getup." She pulled the door open again. She didn't plan to leave, of course. He just had to think she'd leave. Someday, she'd have to write a book on how to work this man to her way of thinking. A few more choice prods to his pride and he'd see the light. "I'm not staying here if you're going to be useless."

The door clapped shut again. She didn't bother hiding her smile. When he lowered his head, expression grim and unbending, she knew she had him. "You know what? Luke's completely wrong about you. You're the most damnably female woman I've ever met."

"Thank you."

"It wasn't a compliment." *How dumb does he think I am?*

"Keep the hair if you must, but the style and the dress have to go."

"Are you ordering me to strip?"

His mouth curved into a dry grin. "Not even if you were a natural blonde, honey."

She smirked. While he and Luke were about as much alike as dogs and cats, the one thing they had in common was their taste in women. Perhaps liking blondes was just a guy thing. She'd have to look into it.

"If we're going to make this work, one thing has to change before anything else."

"Yeah, what?"

"You have to stop looking at me the way a friend does and start seeing me the way a man would."

He should have gotten a beer at May Belle's before they left. Hell, it wouldn't matter. He needed a shot glass for that last comment.

"Burke?"

He had a hot flash of her standing in his tub, wearing nothing but bubbles and water. She'd been all woman to him then, but damn if he was ever going to admit *that.* "Okay, maybe I don't see you that way, but I don't think changing my perception is a good idea."

"Too bad."

Burke finally understood why cavemen hit women over the head with logs.

"Let's start with my name."

"What's wrong with your name?" Good Lord, if she wanted to change it to something debutantish, like Muffy, Buffy or some such crap, this bet was already lost.

"Nothing is wrong with it. You never *use* it. No one does. CB is sexless."

"Are we back to the Cassandra thing?"

She frowned, tilting her head to the left. Great, he forgot she didn't remember her drunken night. "What Cassandra thing?"

"It was nothing." Actually, it was a big fat something only now starting to come into focus for him. Was the whack job Luke did on her self-esteem worse than what she did to his face? "You want me to call you Cassandra now?"

"Cass will do fine. What Cassandra thing?"

Dog. Bone. CB.

"It was nothing." He smiled his most winning charmer. "How about I drive you home? We can get started tomorrow."

She frowned harder, furrowing her brow into three deep grooves, her eyes turning the dark ivy color he associated with her extreme displeasure. Good, he hated being the only one without pleasure. "Why are you suddenly so accommodating?"

He'd have to think up some way to train the suspicious nature out of her. It wouldn't be easy, her radar on lies and deflections was almost never wrong. Except with Luke. "Because your face is breaking out a little more and you probably don't want me seeing you like this. Most women wouldn't," he added for effect. She seemed to be waiting for something else. "Cass?" he guessed and she smiled.

Damn. The name felt awkward on his tongue, but if it got her out of his hair for a little while, he'd call her whatever she wanted.

Cass went pretty willingly if she said so herself. She even let Burke open her door for her. Sure, she had to wait in the cold while he started the engine before he realized she wasn't inside yet, but he did it. He grumbled, but he did it. Sitting in his oversize SUV always made her happy. The plush leather, the polished interior, his subtle scent and a smooth ride—all of it made for an experience she didn't get with her own vehicles. Her work required a truck of her own, but no amount of cleaning could get the smell of fertilizer out of the rugs. She loved the Z, her off-hours car, but for entirely different reasons. It had speed. It had style. Burke designed the interior just for her. It represented freedom. Giving it to Luke would mean a lot more than most people would understand. All the same, nothing was like riding with Burke.

He didn't say a word, driving as if on automatic, his eyes narrowed with his familiar contemplative glare. He was plotting. For once in her life, she was excited about that.

The final turn home was routine except for one thing. Burke pulled a U-ey like a bat out of hell.

"What are you doing?" she all but screeched.

"I got an idea." There was a rash of honking horns and veering cars—including theirs—but within seconds, he was driving back down the main road. "There are a bunch of things about women I can't teach you. I can show you what men like, but unless you see examples you won't have a clue what I'm talking about. So, you're getting some homework."

"Goody." Only Burke could find a way to make homework out of this situation.

"You're the one who wants a new life, Cinderella."

"Cassandra, thank you." Her third grade teacher would be proud to hear the prim notes of her voice. The snarky old bat wouldn't believe it, but she'd be proud all the same. "And another thing," Burke all but pontificated. "Manners. You'll need to see some feminine manners."

"I have manners!"

He leveled a sharp sideways glare at her. "*Why* does Luke have a broken nose?"

All right, he had a *slight* point.

"We're starting from scratch." That didn't sound good.

It sounded worse when he pulled into Enterprising Ernie's Liquor and Video. Burke wasted no time getting out. He didn't seem to think opening her door for her was worth wasting time on either. Curious—but not curious enough to show anyone her rash—she watched him go in and talk to the kid behind the counter.

Too far away to read lips, she tried to decipher gestures and points. When he used the universal symbol of a curvy woman, the cashier got very excited and Cass wondered if he dragged her out here because he had an overwhelming need for porn. Not likely, but hey, she always did say Burke thought too much.

Fifteen minutes later, he came out with two large bags of plastic encased videos. He shoved the bags her way and started up the SUV. "I want you to watch as many of those as you can tonight and tomorrow."

"What?" There had to be fifteen films in her lap!

"Watch them. Watch the women, see how they move, how they talk, what they act like."

"*Tonight?*"

"Tonight." His tone brooked no argument. "All night. Every night until we get it right."

"You watching them with me?" At least they could have popcorn and make fun of the movies together.

"Not this time. I've got to make arrangements."

"For what?" It wasn't like she was going to need a crane or anything.

"Leave it to me."

Cass reached into the bag. "*I Was A Male War Bride, North By Northwest, How to Marry a Millionaire, Niagra. Gentlemen Prefer Blondes?*" Yeah, real surprise. "What are these?"

"Movies."

"*Old* movies?"

If she didn't know better, she'd swear he was grinning. "Everything is old at Ernie's."

"You know I don't watch black and white. *You* don't even watch black and white. And these better not be musicals."

"Actually, I don't know. I asked the kid, she seemed to know what I was looking for."

"I'll bet." Kid or not, every girl but her who made basic eye contact with Burke Halifax magically lost all communication with her brain. It never failed. Cass put the movies back in the bag. She had a feeling she'd rather he got porn.

Five minutes after Burke dropped her off at home, Cass finally gave in to the inevitable. With Burke, she'd bluffed about her family. They weren't likely to take her makeover any better than Burke had. Eddie might ask her if she were trying to get raped and Hayne would make jokes until his voice ran out. It was too cold to stay out on the porch with only two bags of movies to keep her warm. She opened the door to the familiar smell of Hayne's beef stew, her father's popcorn and the sounds of *Wheel of Fortune*.

In the twenty-five years since Lora Bishop's death, almost nothing in the old two-story had changed. The paint—while retouched over the years—was still the same beige, the couches were still the same not-so-comfortable tweed and the carpet was the same brown, green and orange not-so-shaggy shag. The pictures still hung in the same spots or sat on the same shelves. Knickknacks had yet to be rearranged, habits had yet to be removed. Her father still fell asleep on his beaten recliner. Hayne still left his jacket on the banister knob. Sometimes it was nice to be home.

Now wasn't one of those times.

"Hey CB, that you?" Hayne's voice called from the kitchen, accompanied by a clattering of pots. "Was wondering when you were coming home. Heard you tied one on at Shaky Jake's—" He walked out of the kitchen in mid-laugh, which turned into mid-choke at the sight of her.

Cass smiled weakly. She heard the squeak indicating her father was turning in his chair and swung her gaze toward him.

"Holy—"

"What in the hell happened to you?"

Ah, the sound of appreciative men. "I…um…had an allergic reaction."

"To what? Dad, look at her hair!"

"I'm looking, son." Eddie stood up, something resembling a smile pulling at his sun-browned mouth. "Is that a dress?"

This was positive. A tremulous smile forming without her permission, Cass dumped the bag of videos over the back of the couch and did a quick turn for him. "May Belle gave it to me. She said it was one of hers back when she was a starlet in Hollywood."

"Explains all the room at the top," Hayne snickered, leaning a shoulder against the corner of the kitchen wall and crossing his arms across his too wide chest.

Cass wished she still had one of May Belle's shoes. She'd throw it at him. "Shut up."

"Wouldn't your mama have loved to see you like this," her father went on, oblivious as always to their bickering. "Look at you, all prettied up!"

Cass's irritation with her brother melted away at Eddie Bishop's shining eyes. He crossed the room and wrapped his big arms around her in a bear hug. She was used to those, her father felt better about hugs than he did about most other mushy emotions. She patted his still hard back as best she could.

"You almost look like her, with your hair like that, 'cept you got a little too much Bishop on the nose." He pulled away, looking down at her with deeper assessment. "Hey, what happened to your face?"

Cass felt her cheeks flame. "Allergy, remember?"

Eddie nodded. Then he smacked her shoulder the way he would have on any other night. "Where've you been?"

Just like that, back to normal. Cass wasn't sure whether to be annoyed or relieved. She headed for the stairs, hoping to put on something a little more comfortable and with a lot less draft, but Hayne answered for her and stopped her dead in her tracks.

"She's been hiding out at Burke's. Don't worry, she was safe."

Turning around, she watched her father settle back into the chair and the Wheel and Hayne go back to stinking up the kitchen by over-spicing the food. "What do you mean *safe?*"

Hayne didn't bother to turn away from his giant pot. "What do you mean, what do I mean? I mean safe. You were at Burke's, for Pete's sake. What could have happened to you there?"

Cass wrinkled her nose. Geez, how dumb *were* they? "You heard yourself, I was three sheets to the wind the other night. Anything could have happened."

"Yeah," Hayne laughed, his annoying older-brother, I-know-everything laugh. "Like what?"

"I don't know. Something!" She thought about Luke's assumption. "I...I could have slept with him. We could be having a wild, rampaging affair!"

Eddie turned up the volume on the television. Cass spared him a look while he positioned his glasses on the end of his nose so he could see Vanna a little clearer.

"I could be wickedly having my way with him. I could have done a lot of things, you know."

"Yeah," Hayne said, stirring his sauce and all but ignoring her. "But you aren't."

"How do you know?"

"Because you're talking about Burke and we're also talking about *you*. 'Nuff said."

Stomping into the kitchen, Cass poked him in his ticklish rib. And not lightly. "No, not enough said. I could seduce him. I could seduce anyone in this town if I wanted to. In fact, how do you know I haven't?"

Her brother squirmed away from her invading index finger, guarding his weakness with one of his too big biceps, frowning at her like she'd lost her mind. "I know because Burke wouldn't touch you with a ten foot sewer pipe. As for you screwing around with anyone else, I know because all you've ever done is come home and fall in your bed with your boots on. In this town, we'd have heard about it before your undies were done twisting. Face it, you're too tired for men."

"I wasn't too tired for Luke."

"Look where *that* got you." Hayne raised a superior dark eyebrow while gesturing with his stirring spoon. "Living with a guy who didn't know which end was up. I told you he was no good. Burke told you a thousand times. Even Dad told you and when was the last time he noticed who we were dating?"

Cass rolled her eyes. "Who *you* were dating, you mean." *Hayne* barely knew half the time.

"Either way," he continued, "we all know you haven't been with anyone since Luke. You might as well go upstairs and get out of that outfit. You look funny that way."

"You better get used to it, because I'm staying this way."

Hayne scoffed. "Yeah, right. I bet you didn't even know how to put that dress on without May Belle to figure it out for you."

"Well, I'm learning, okay? And while we're having this little conversation, it's about time you stopped calling me CB. My name is Cassandra. Or call me Cass. I'm not responding to CB anymore."

Hayne shrugged, seeing to his food. "Sure, whatever, CB."

She slugged his arm, nearly bumping him off balance. "I mean it. I'm going to be treated like a girl around here, do you understand, you over-muscled schmuck?"

He laughed. "Well, you hit like a girl."

"At least I don't scream like one." She turned on her heel and went out to the living room for her bags of movies. As she stomped up the steps, determined to make enough noise to annoy even her father, she heard Hayne's voice call after her.

"If you're the resident girl, does that mean you're doing all the cooking and cleaning from now on?"

Rather than dignify that with an answer, she slammed her door to show her irritation. Twice.

It was official. Burke was off his rocker. And he had a bad thing for blondes. Real bad.

Three in the morning and Cass was staring one-eyed at the small television on her five-drawer dresser. The other eye was sleeping, along with her cold feet and the hand she was laying her face on. She wanted to sleep so badly. No, she wanted to put on a pair of sweats and eat some food—whose smell permeated her bedroom hours ago.

She had refused to change her dress simply out of stubbornness. Refusing to come down and eat dinner was sheer stupidity. They all knew she had to eat. She had the metabolism of a moose, according to her father. She'd stopped paying any attention to Lauren Bacall's plan to bag a rich, old guy a long time ago, instead imagining thick chunks of beef, soft, flavorful vegetables and hearty brown sauce.

She couldn't take anymore. Getting up and walking as softly as possible down the hall to the stairs, she made it to the kitchen where everything was clean and put away. Her father's snores from the recliner covered the smacking sound of the refrigerator's seal breaking while she opened the door. Surprised, she stared inside at the bowl covered with cling wrap, a piece of paper on top of it: *"Knew you'd be hungry."*

Smirking and grateful without wanting to admit it, Cass pulled out the large bowl and transferred it to the microwave. After setting the time, she leaned against the fridge and sighed.

In only one day, she'd heard four different opinions on what made a woman feminine. Five, if you counted what Burke said *wouldn't*. May Belle seemed to think femininity was found in using a beautiful surface to compete with men. Lola thought it was using beauty to seduce them. The video girl apparently thought it was in speedy repartee and high glamour. Hayne… Cass snorted while the microwave dinged. Hayne thought femininity was either the inability to take care of oneself or an undying urge to take care of everyone else by cooking and cleaning. But Burke…

She dipped her fork into her bowl.

What would draw *him* to a woman? What did he find irresistible? She tried to think back on any of the women he dated, but none stuck in her mind. All that really came to mind was a haze of big hair and big eyes. He didn't have too much of a type except slightly easy. Never anyone particularly skeevy, but not anyone you'd mistake for a brain surgeon, either.

How could she be his best friend and not have a clue what he looked for in a woman? Somehow, she knew if she were going to get through this, she'd have to figure it out.

Chapter Five

Morning came in haze of voices and light, neither of which Cass was happy to have in her bedroom. She lifted her face from the flannel-encased pillow and looked over at the television. When the dance scene between Ginger Rodgers and Fred Astaire in roller skates made itself clear to her foggy eyes, she realized the built-in VCR was set to rewind and repeat. Wondering how many times the film had done it while she slept, she checked her watch and groaned. Only once!

Since raising her hand to find the remote was too much energy to waste, Cass buried her face back in the pillows and ignored it. At least, until the heavy pounding on her door signaled Hayne was awake.

"Hey, CB, move it or lose it! You got ten minutes to eat breakfast before we head out to the Wild Oaks property!"

God, to not work with her family would have been such a blessing. For precious seconds, Cass fantasized about working a late shift at Enterprising Ernie's instead of doing the early one for Bishop Landscaping and Nursery. No Hayne waking her up at the crack—she checked her watch again—no, the *inception* of dawn. No Dad asking her to do the bookkeeping because he wouldn't hire an accountant. No creating floral arrangements for other people's weddings even if it did bring in a lot of revenue. No one calling her Little Miss Mud Pie.

"I quit!" she yelled as loud as she could through her pillow.

Hayne laughed. "See you in five!"

Unwillingly, she pried herself out of the warm blankets and stumbled into the bathroom her father had built when she was fourteen. It was the one concession to her sex in the Bishop household. Fact was, when her breasts finally decided to show up, it was pretty disconcerting to have her brother walk in on her shower. Worse, her father. The Bishop men weren't quite known for their ability to knock.

She stripped out of the sweats she finally allowed herself after eating last night and climbed into the stall, moaning at the warmth of the hot water pouring over her. It took all her strength not to stay in there for more time than it took to get clean. When she stepped out, wrapped in a towel, it was to face her unfamiliar reflection in the mirror.

She stopped dead, blinking at the stranger before her. Who *was* that? Long, auburn hair slicked back from her face, tanned with a few freckles here and there. With steam still wisping around her, Cass stepped closer and peered at her face. The welts were gone, thank God, leaving her fresh and rosy from the heat of the water. Her own eyes glowed back at her, more vivid now with her hair brighter.

Curious, she leaned away from the glass and allowed her towel to slide away. Truthfully, not much had changed in respect to her body, but something looked different in a major way. Her gaze traveled over her slim build, studying the curves she often forgot about. True, she wasn't the bustiest pers—*woman* in town, but she wasn't tiny. Bigger than a couple of others she knew, now that she really looked. The shape wasn't bad, either. They didn't sag, anyway. There were women who'd kill for that much. She'd seen the surgical shows her brother watched when he was hard up to see a boob or two.

All the physical work she did pruning trees, carrying and laying sod, not to mention the demands made in the nursery at least had the benefit of keeping her fit. She was toned quite well; if someone slicked her up she'd look like one of those fitness magazine cover girls. She hadn't thought much about it because those girls wore as close to nothing as they could get away with and most of her clothes were T-shirts and jeans. Sometimes she wore shorts, but not often.

Picking up her towel, she wandered out of the bathroom and over to her closet. Looking from hanger to hanger, there wasn't a single thing in there she wanted to be. The clothes screamed "Ignore me!" as loud as they could. All her shirts were too big, chosen for opportunity rather than taste. In the back was a church dress she wore to a funeral a few years ago. It was simple, black and shapeless. It was right next to the still shrouded wedding dress she never got to wear. That thing would be the first to go. Come to think of it, the first chance she got, *all* of this was going to Goodwill or to the trash. Maybe a few things tossed into the incinerator at the nursery, for kicks.

Getting dressed simply because she had to, she put on the essentials, a standard set of jeans and an old T-shirt. Grabbing a hat, she stuffed her hair into it and pulled her checkbook from her dresser drawer. She needed to find clothes screaming something she *did* want to be. It was time for a change.

"What do you mean you're not coming in today? Who's gonna come with me to Wild Oaks?" Hayne stared at her while the truck warmed up.

She sipped at a mugful of coffee. "I have some errands to run and they can't be put off anymore."

"Why not?"

She turned to him with an expression of exasperation. "Because I've put them off all my life and they're getting done today, okay? In fact, I'm taking my vacation."

"*What?*"

"Vacation. You know, when you don't come into work for two weeks because you've earned time off slaving for your family?"

"Is this about the hair thing?" Hayne wasn't mean. To anyone else, he was a reasonable, thoughtful person. Probably. But they'd spent their lives pretending they were still twelve-years-old and he didn't have the first clue how to be tactful with her. He especially had no idea what it felt like to be uncomfortable in his skin. Black hair falling forward over his forehead, hazel eyes with short dark lashes, a kind of all-day stubble that never went away, he fit in everywhere he went, in whatever company. He would never understand how important these changes would be to her. The thought of trying to explain it made her head hurt.

"Partially. Please, Hayne. I know you're going to hear about it later from someone, and you deserve to know but I don't want to go into it right now, okay?"

He stared at her, his mouth tight, jaw working left to right, reminding her of all the times when they were kids and the other girls didn't want to play with her. Once a big brother, always a big brother. He didn't like it, but he didn't try to bully her. "You're gonna tell me some time, though, right?"

Cass nodded. If it wouldn't result in more hives, she'd hug him.

"Okay," he said, expelling his breath, putting the truck in gear and pulling out of the driveway. "Where to?"

"Drop me off at Shaky Jake's. Burke left my car there last night."

"Do I get to hear why?"

"No."

He huffed a little, but he kept driving.

"Uh-oh," she groaned not too long later, scrunching her face at the sight of the restaurant. A crowd around her car was not a good sign. Hayne saw it too and instead of dropping her off, parked in the lot. Cass climbed out of the cab and slammed the door, garnering some attention from the people on the outer edge of the circle. She waited for Hayne to catch up while the men elbowed each other enough to part for her.

Her knot of dread tightened when she recognized a couple of them from Luke's party the night before. None of them recognized her, though. She doubted they'd recognize their own mothers, most of them bleary eyed. Still, they separated and opened a path to her car.

Where Luke was taking Polaroids.

"What the hell are you doing?" she asked, hands on her hips.

"Better yet, what the hell are you doing *here*?" Hayne demanded.

Luke put the camera away from his face, pulling the last shot from the mouth of the instant camera and waving it. He smiled as if old friends had joined the party. "Taking pictures of my car."

"Your *what*?"

Cass winced. Hayne hit a new decibel, not to mention a new key for his usually baritone voice. She should have caught him up when she had the chance.

"My car." Luke pronounced the words as if they were phonics tools. "What's the matter, Hayne, sister dear didn't tell you I was back in town?"

Cass felt Hayne's hot glare on the top of her head for a short moment. "No, but it sure as hell looks like she said hello."

Luke shrugged. "She sucker punched me."

Hayne snorted, then turned on the bystanders. "What do you all think you're looking at? Get out of here. And you," he turned back to Luke with a threatening finger, "get away from our property."

"For now," Luke replied amicably, still flashing his picture. Faking an afterthought, he tossed it back at them. "Keep it. Don't want you forgetting what it looks like."

Cass watched him join his friends and head to their cars on the other side of the lot.

"What was he talking about? Why does that assmunch think he's going to lay one finger on this car?"

Cass looked up at her brother's thunderous expression and sighed. She wasn't getting out of this without an explanation and she knew it. While Luke and his buddies drove away, she detailed the breaking of the nose, the wedding plans and finally the bet. He groaned at that.

"You're turning yourself inside-out over *Luke? Again?*"

Cass shook her head. Why did both Hayne and Burke have it in their heads that she would willingly do anything for Luke ever again? Had she ever changed anything for him before? No. Her only fault had been believing he cared about her. Those days were long gone. "I'm doing this for *me*. Luke just happens to be a bonus."

"Yeah? How?"

She looked down at the picture of her car and crunched it into the gravel with her boot. "Because it's going to feel so good to rub his face in it when I win."

"I probably shouldn't ask why you thought of me to help you shop," Alice Panyon said as she nibbled on a Godiva chocolate. She pushed the stroller in front of her with her free hand, oblivious to the fact that her belly could do it for her. "But I'm going to."

Cass smiled at her, holding several bags in one hand and licking an ice cream cone with the other. The way the North County Mall was situated, there was always something to eat in between stores. Reva—Alice and Sel's two-year-old daughter—was working her way through a giant pretzel, content to lie back in the stroller and watch the world go by.

Perhaps a compliment would sidestep the conversation. "You have style?"

"Uh-huh, but that's not it."

Cass shrugged. It wasn't like Alice hadn't figured it out already. "You're probably the only person in town with an inkling of what it's like to be me."

Alice didn't laugh, but she could have. Aside from having a similar height of around five-nine, Alice was definitely day to Cass's night. With her pale blonde hair falling to the middle of her back, a normally willowy figure, angelic face and perfect manners, Alice didn't exactly have tomboy written all over her. But ten years as a firefighter hadn't happened by accident. She was stronger than some men, did work some still argued was no place for a woman and had to fight town opinion for more years than even Cass liked to think about. But when she retired, it had nothing to do with anyone else's opinion. Alice did things when she was good and ready and not one second before. Cass admired that kind of strength. She certainly didn't have it.

"There are worse things to be than you, Cass." Alice's quiet reminder didn't have the teasing quality her voice usually held. She sounded serious.

"Sure there are." Murderers, rapists, lounge singers. "That doesn't mean I want to be Little Miss Mud Pie forever."

Alice chuckled, her smoky voice full of warmth. "Well, if the damage we've done to your credit card is any indication, you won't be."

Cass smiled again. Okay, she would have to work the rest of her life to pay off most of what she'd bought, but it was worth it. Seeing her own reflection in the mirror and liking it was addicting. For the first time in her life, she understood why other women enjoyed shopping. Seeing Alice's eyes light up with sisterly surprise gave her courage to try outfits she would never have dared otherwise. Even hearing Reva's excited clapping had gone toward proving she was making the right decision. Now all she had to do was pass Burke's inspection.

"Burke's inspection?"

Shoot, did I say that out loud? "Um, yeah. He's helping me with this…makeover."

"I'm guessing you won the poker game?" Alice waggled her eyebrows.

Cass frowned. "Yeah, but he didn't agree to help me until he ran into Luke himself."

"Oh," Alice said, her expression dimming.

"What's that 'oh' about?"

"I hoped Burke would finally buy a clue and take you up on your offer, I guess."

Cass stopped walking, tilting her head to the side and inspecting her friend for pregnancy-induced insanity. "What offer? Why would he need to buy a clue?"

"You're kidding, right?" Alice stopped pushing the stroller, her mouth forming an "o" while her eyes widened. "Oh, my God, you're not kidding. You seriously don't know?"

"Don't know what?"

"You and Burke are…well, that the two of you are…" Alice twirled her hand as if it would clear things up for Cass. It didn't. Finally, she sighed and rolled her eyes. "You guys are in love with each other."

Definitely pregnancy-induced insanity. "Are you nuts?" Cass sputtered, choking on her ice cream and a peal of laughter. "Me and Burke?" *Yeah and aliens landed on the Statue of Liberty.*

"Of course you and Burke. Everyone knows how you feel about him. Burke probably doesn't, but he's a typical man. You'll have to practically write a sign on your forehead for him to get it."

How she felt? "Everyone is wrong." *Dead wrong. Colossally wrong.* "Burke is my friend—"

"Uh-huh."

"I'm not in love with him, Alice."

"Uh-huh."

"I'm not."

"Sure."

"Stop agreeing with me, already!" Cass brought her hands to her fiery cheeks while Alice giggled into another bite of chocolate.

"Okay."

Cass sighed, trying not to smile, but Alice's eyes were dancing, making it hard to even feign anger. "Seriously! I'm not. He's my *friend*. It's all he's ever been. Even if I was—" she thought of her brother's offhand comment, which sobered her right up, "—Burke wouldn't touch me with a ten foot sewer pipe."

Alice slipped her a sideways glance of disbelief. . "Burke is a man, honey. You have a great figure and you know him better than he knows himself. Trust me, if you gave him a push in the right direction, he'd be begging to touch you."

Cass snickered. "Yeah, right." Burke didn't beg. Period. She could be the image of his wettest dream and it wouldn't happen.

"Really. He would. If what Ben Friedly told me last night is true, you won't need to push real hard either."

Cass's ears perked. "Why? What did Ben tell you?"

"That Burke looked ready to eat you alive in the bar in front of half the town. In a good way," Alice added, probably because Burke eating people alive usually involved yelling, insults and occasionally violence.

Cass tried to remember something out of the ordinary happening at the bar. All she could think of was the moment he washed her face. *She* was the one who'd gotten all soft and gooey, for once understanding why every girl in town had a crush on her best friend. You couldn't be close to someone with eyes that intense, features that strong and a touch that gentle, without losing yourself for a moment. Or two. Okay, three, but that was it.

"I say you get yourself all dolled up and give it a shot."

Cass blinked out of her reverie. "Give what a shot?"

"Seducing Burke. Give it a try."

Who would have guessed speechlessness physically hurt? Cass tried to make a sound. Nothing came out. She tried to breathe, but the two mental directives blocked each other and she ended up choking to the point of tears. Alice whacked her on the back until Cass finally got a grip on her disbelief.

"I can't seduce Burke!"

A few people stopped to stare at her. Cass glared until they went away.

Alice just looked amused. "Sure you can. You stroll up to him, kiss him as if your life depended on it and see what happens."

"He'd kill me is what would happen." Painfully.

Alice wrinkled her nose. "If you want to pull off this transformation of yours, Cass, you're going to have to do more than dive-bomb your credit card."

"Hey!" This was beyond dive-bombing. Her card looked like a pack of wolves gnawed it.

"Hey what? Do you want to know the true secret of feeling feminine or not?"

Cass gave up arguing.

"Femininity is about more than clothes or hair or make-up. It's not high heels or cooking or lingerie. It's about people *seeing* you're a girl. Not you changing how you dress and telling them to. That won't work. You'll still be CB Bishop, dressed different.

"The reason you don't feel like a girl isn't because you aren't one. It's not because everyone sees you a certain way. It's because *you* don't see *yourself* a certain way. You don't know your own sensuality and until you do, nothing we bought today is going to create it for you."

"I have to seduce Burke if I'm going to be feminine?" Her head throbbed. *Yet another definition to remember.*

"No, sex won't do it either."

"But you just said—"

"Femininity is a spark, Cass." Alice's brow creased, her voice authoritative. "It's the...*thing* that makes you realize you're soft where he's not. The thing about you that makes *him* realize it, too. Sometimes being feminine is believing you can seduce any man in any room at any time. Even if you don't, you have to believe you can."

"Only sometimes?"

Alice shrugged.

This is important, Cass wanted to yell. *My head isn't* that *hard to get through!* Instead, she waited, breath held, for Alice to continue.

"Sometimes, it's the way you feel when you hold your baby. Or when another woman says you look nice. Sometimes, it's a simple as believing in yourself and the rest follows naturally. I know you don't want to hear this, but Burke was right to tell you you'd know it when you see it. You'll know it when you feel it."

That's it? "But I *can't* feel it. Why else do you think I'm doing all this?" The frustration made Cass want to hit something. Or kick something. Neither the little girl in the stroller or the woman with the belly were acceptable targets, meaning she had to buck up and deal. Alice nibbled her candy, watching while Cass tried to fit this new information in with the other confusing pieces.

They stood looking at each other for a while, silent while the mall hummed around them. People walked this way and that, moving from store to store as if something important weren't happening in front of them. For Cass, the only thing clicking was resentment.

"You're like everyone else, aren't you? You think I'm doing this because of Luke. Like I want him back or something."

"Truthfully?"

"Yeah, truthfully."

"I think you're doing it for Burke."

Cass laughed, but it felt almost as hollow as it sounded. "Burke is the last person who wants me to change. If you heard some of our arguments..." She laughed again, which didn't make any sense because she had the strangest urge to cry. "I'm doing this for *me*, Alice. If Burke had his way, I'd be Little Miss Mud Pie forever."

Though Alice's eyes gleamed, she nodded her head. "That's a big first step, Cass. Makes me think you might pull this off."

"Because I'm not doing it for Burke?"

"Because you should never change for anyone else."

Cass's smile came easier this time.

Alice gestured for them to continue walking when Reva's mad rocking of the stroller finally got her attention. "I still think you should set your sights on someone. Like target practice. It might help."

She imagined walking into a roomful of men with her father's old rifle. "Oh sure, that'll work. What am I supposed to do if I catch him?"

Alice's mischievous eyebrow wiggling set them both off on a rail of giggling.

"I'm serious! The last thing I need is another man in my life. I've got plenty, thanks."

"No one said you have to keep them. You walk into a room like you own every single man you see. Even the married ones." Alice stopped walking, putting a hand on Cass's sleeve to make her look. "Lift your chin. Roll your shoulders back. Look down at them. Never let them think you're happy to see any of them. Look at a man once, never look back unless *he* comes to *you*."

Cass stared, wide-eyed. Right in front of her, Alice had gone from mini-van mom to runway model. Her eyes had gone smoky and half-lidded, a blank expression of disinterest smoothing her features. Without so much as a flip of her ponytail or a fluff of her a-line kerchief blouse, she'd changed into someone Cass wouldn't have recognized. A blink later it was gone and Alice's impish grin was back. "See?"

"How did you do that?"

"Easy. I believed there wasn't a man in this mall who wouldn't think I'm sexy." She patted her belly. "You'd be surprised how many guys think pregnancy is hot. You can do it. Just believe in yourself a little."

"Believe." Cass tried to picture it as she walked. When she walked into rooms, no one noticed but Burke and usually only because he was waiting for her. The thought of trying to get everyone's attention the way Alice recommended made her face start itching again. When Luke's friends hit on her at Shaky Jakes, she'd tried to be excited and thrilled to have so much attention, but in truth, the men had frightened her. Too many eyes lingered on her breasts, too many hands trying to pull on hers. The things they'd said, some trying to be alluring, a few straight out crude. No, remembering that, she didn't want to be in a room full of men *without* her father's old rifle.

The only man she could imagine targeting and still being safe with was Burke. She'd be safe with Burke in any situation. But could she really try to seduce him? She tried to see herself tempting her friend. It didn't work. She kept imagining him either laughing or getting mad at her. Mostly the latter. Like she'd told him before, until he saw her as a woman instead of a friend, he was no good to her and Burke would never look at her any different.

Except…

She remembered the look on his face the night before in the bar, his fingertip moving over the edge of her bottom lip. Nothing clinical existed in that burning touch. She shivered anew, her lip tingling under the remembered caress. His eyes simmered. He stared at her lip like some kind of tasty treat. Heat billowed low in her belly, drowning automatic denial. He'd forgotten for a moment what she was to him. For one suspended second, she was a woman and he was a man. If he could forget once…couldn't he forget again?

"Thatta girl," Alice murmured. "I almost feel bad for Burke."

Cass blinked out of the reverie. "What? Why?"

"Poor man won't know what truck hit him." Alice shushed Cass's worry away with a wave of her hand. "That's a good thing, trust me. Now, have you decided what make-up is best for you yet?"

Cass cringed, all ideas of seduction melting to a puddle at her feet. "Um, May Belle helped me already; I'm all set."

Alice inspected her face. "Why aren't you wearing any?"

She considered lying, but it wouldn't work. Alice knew all her tells. "If I put any of it on, I look like the last survivor of a bee cult's sacrificial offering."

Alice laughed, covering her mouth. "I'm sorry. I should have warned you about May's homemade make-up. Come on, one more stop. My treat."

"But—"

"No buts. Call it a gift or don't, but there's no way I'm letting May Belle get another crack at those eyes."

Helplessly, Cass followed Alice's lead. She had no choice. She had the feeling, pregnant to bursting or not, Alice would hunt her down and rope her in if she refused.

"What do you mean you haven't seen her all day? Where is she?" Burke demanded into his phone, slamming his office door at the screeching sound of the metal cutter in the workshop beyond. He listened to Hayne explain Cass was out and he didn't know where she went. "Did she say when she'd be back?"

The screeching sounded behind him again as his shift manager, Rafael Abogada, opened the door with his lunch in hand. He closed it, rushed over to the television and flicked the switch. Immediately, the soothing tones of Oprah's theme song began. 'Fael settled into the chair on the other side of Burke's desk and pulled out his sandwich to eat.

"Is that...*Oprah*?" Hayne asked, making it sound as if he had caught Burke *inflagrante delecti* or something.

"No...yes, it's a commercial." He shrugged at 'Fael's admonishing stare, waving a hand at him to go back to his show. The older man laughed quietly and did as he was gestured. Burke eyed the sandwich half waiting inside the open mini-cooler across the desk. 'Fael's wife had it in her head that her husband's hoagies required three whole farm animals to construct. Meat fluttered out of the French bread slabs, waving at him until he either asked 'Fael for a bite or went stomping to the deli for a pale version of his own. "When you see her, tell her I called. Make sure she knows I'll be waiting for her at my house after work."

He nearly hung up, but he heard Hayne making noises as if he wanted to say something. The sandwich called louder, since 'Fael was making speedy progress into the one in his hands.

"Spit it out, Hayne, I'm busy." He tapped his fingers on the calendar ink blotter atop his desk to prove it.

"Did you...nah, never mind."

"Did I what?" He'd just ask for a bite. One and he'd be fine. Otherwise, he'd have to figure a way to turn his tongue into a meal because he wasn't going to get to the deli any time soon.

"Have you ever slept with Cass?"

Well, look at that. He *could* swallow his own tongue.

"No," he finally said after a few seconds of trying not to choke, sandwich forgotten. He ran his finger over a smudge of oil in the middle of the fifteenth. "But if I had—and I'm not saying I ever did— why would it be any business of yours? Cassie's no kid anymore." Burke congratulated himself for not sounding defensive. Or interested.

"No, she's not," Hayne agreed peaceably enough. "But she's still my sister and you're still my friend, even if you do spend more time with *her* these days." He just had to get that in, didn't he? Burke couldn't dredge up any interest in explaining how he didn't like picking up women every weekend, least of all the sobby, heartbroken ones Hayne found like bad pennies. "It's just something she said."

Burke took his hand off the paper. *She said something about sleeping with me?* "What did she say? Exactly?"

"She was mad, I guess, about this Luke thing."

"You know about that?"

"I'm about the only person in town who didn't, it turns out." Hayne chuckled, sounding proud. "Damn, but she flattened his face, didn't she?"

"Why don't you get back to what she said about me?"

"What? Oh, she claimed she was having a wild, rampaging affair with you or something. I figured she was pulling my leg, but thought I'd ask anyway. Just in case."

Uh-oh. "Just in case what?"

"You know, in case I have to pull out your intestines through your nose or something." He laughed, good and hearty, not noticing Burke was swallowing carefully instead of joining him. "I have to go," Hayne said, abruptly cutting short his own good time. "You wouldn't believe the hot little number who walked in here—"

Burke looked down at the receiver, which started emitting a loud dial tone. He hung up and shook his head at his friend's lack of goodbye. Enough of a reminder for him. Hayne would shoot him if he found out the way Burke had noticed Cass's rounder attributes, so he'd better stop noticing them. The sooner this bet was over with, the sooner they could all go back to the way things used to be.

"It's Tuesday. Relationship Day," 'Fael pointed at the TV above Burke's head with the remnants of his massive sandwich. "You hungry? Chavella made too much again. She says I have to watch my weight but then she gets mad when I don't eat all this food. The *bruja's* crazy, man."

Burke spun in his chair as the psychologist who made the show bearable strolled on stage. Ah, what the hell? 'Fael handed him the cooler and Burke rolled his chair to the other side of his desk. The sandwich wasn't as satisfying as Cass would be, but he could do a lot worse than a good meal and a balding buddy to share it with, couldn't he?

It didn't matter if he couldn't. Cassandra Bishop was officially off-limits. Anything and anyone else was going to feel disappointing. Which should be a relief. He couldn't ruin their relationship with sex if he knew it wasn't going to happen. Besides, 'Fael had the distinct advantage of being a quiet date, something Cass couldn't promise on her best day. That right there put him in Burke's top five.

He bit into the sandwich, determined not to rate Cass at all.

Cass was extra careful as she walked up Burke's porch steps later that night. While the shoes didn't have a stiletto heel like last night's nightmare in black velvet, they were still a good three inches high. Alice called them "platform sandals". Certainly felt like a platform. A damn high one.

Standing in front of the door, she wiggled her toes, pleased at the soft coral color shining back from her pedicured nails. The shade didn't match the periwinkle blue of her dress, but neither did her red goose bumps so she made herself push the doorbell so Burke would let her in. Precious heartbeats went by before she heard the doorknob turn. Warm, gold light arrowed out of the doorway to pool around her. It would have shared some of its heat, but Burke's big shadow stepped in the way.

"Where the hell have you been?"

Cass motioned to enter the house and Burke grumbled something before pushing the door open wider, allowing her to pass. She continued her careful steps to the living room, holding on to her wicker basket as if it alone could do what she came here for.

I can do this, I can do this, I can do this...

"Stop scrunching up your face, you look like a three-year-old."

"Stop scolding me like I'm a three-year-old." He was ruining this whole thing.

"You're late."

"We never set a time."

"You're dressed wrong."

"I'm dressed fine. I even had help." She put her hands on her hips. From the way his inky hair seemed to stand on end, his mouth carved into a grim line, his hands in fists beneath the rolled up shirtsleeves, the man was absolutely livid. "What are you so mad about?"

"You wanted me to show you how to...do whatever it is you're doing and you keep going off and doing stuff to yourself without asking me first."

"I'm getting the easy stuff out of the way!" She tossed her basket on the couch, getting upset herself. "The things we need."

"You don't *need* a dress that short!"

Cass looked down. Was that what he was yelling about? She thought it was cute. So did Alice. Soft blue, with lace at the neckline and blue ribbon winding just under her breasts, the little outfit made the most of what she had to show off. Her favorite part was the flippy hem, the way it jumped this way and that made her want to wiggle just to see it go. "It's a summer dress. They're supposed to be short."

"I can see your thighs!"

She raised an eyebrow and he stopped trying to argue. Instead, he pulled the white dishtowel off his shoulder and turned on his heel.

"I've got dishes to put away."

"I'll help—"

"No, you won't. You'll stay right there and you won't say a single word. I'll be back when I'm done and we'll get to work."

"Yes, master," she grumbled.

"Better."

Cass let him leave, flounced into the soft pillows of the couch and didn't care in the slightest where the skirt folds landed. The man was as dumb as a rock. Of course it was short! It was a typical girly dress, like all the ones she hadn't gotten to wear growing up. The stockings were silk, like whispers instead of fabric, and they were the most delicate things she'd ever touched. Alice showed her to wear special white gloves when she handled them so she wouldn't snag them with the calluses on her hands.

Together, they spent hours finding make-up that didn't set her on fire and Alice taught her how to put it on. She didn't even need foundation, according to the woman she was voting into sainthood. Alice also showed her how to make her eyes look darker, more striking, and oddly enough, it worked.

Or at least, it would have if Burke weren't completely impenetrable. The jerk. Cass crossed her legs the way she'd seen the

Almighty Marilyn do it and mentally stuck her tongue out at the man in the kitchen. At least she'd picked up *that* much from the movies.

All the dishes were put away by the time Cass arrived, so Burke didn't know how long he was going to be able to hide in the kitchen. And he didn't in the slightest feel bad about hiding. It was the only thing a man could do when overcome by a libido completely without sense. Opening the door to Cass was like discovering the most erotic Christmas ever, in the middle of April.

She wasn't supposed to have legs that went on for miles. They certainly weren't supposed to be shapely and exposed. Even May Belle's dress was of a sensible length. This little blue number had no idea what the meaning of sensibility was. Or gravity, for that matter. He bet if she bent over at all, anyone behind her would think it was Christmas, too.

He filled a glass with water straight from the tap and gulped it down.

It wasn't enough. Nothing short of tearing her dress off with his teeth would be. But he couldn't do it. Hayne made his opinion clear; meaning Eddie probably had the same one. The line in the sand was drawn. A man did not sleep with his friend, especially not a man like him, one utterly incapable of caring for a woman outside of the bedroom. He couldn't treat Cass that way. He would not touch the friend. No licking the friend, either. If he could get away with not looking at her, he'd do it.

First things first, he was going through her new wardrobe and would probably throw away half of it. She'd only need the clothes for a few weeks anyway. Afterward, she'd go back to being his favorite couch potato, a loudmouth armchair quarterback.

Little Miss Mud Pie. Little Miss Mud Pie. Little Miss Mud Pie.

He kept repeating the phrase in his head as he put the glass on the drainboard and went into the living room. He circled the couch, feeling much better prepared to deal with her, even willing to smile about this idiocy. Until he saw her.

This *wasn't* Little Miss Mud Pie.

This was Miss Scorching August.

Miss Coconut Body Oil.

Miss Ride 'em, Cowboy.

For the first time in his life, he wished he didn't wear boots.

"Burke?" She turned those glittering green eyes on him, her irritation having flushed her cheeks. She'd been chewing on her bottom lip again, he could tell. It was wet. Pink. Pouty.

He forced his eyes to look for safer ground. Why couldn't he find any?

She couldn't know her skirt lay high enough on her thigh that he could see the lacy tops of her stockings. Who wore garter belts these days? Who knew he liked them? Especially pale, pale blue ones, with tiny satin flowers on the straps where the clasp held onto the lace.

"Burke?" She shifted, thank God, pivoting in her seat and leaning forward. Then he realized the heart-shaped top of her dress didn't come up nearly enough. The shadow or nipple question reared its ugly head again. What? Wasn't there enough fabric to make a whole dress?

"Cass?"

She brightened at the use of her name. She braced her weight forward onto her arms, pressing her breasts together, answering the nipple question with strawberry clarity.

"We need to get you out of that thing," he said, closing his eyes and wiping the beginning of sweat from his brow. *Do not look. For the love of God, don't look.*

"What?"

"The dress. It has to go." He opened his eyes. He was only human. Even he had to admit there were times when he was weak. Not that he felt good about it. Especially not when she smiled as if he told her she won a jackpot.

"You want me to take off my dress?"

Why doesn't that sound like what I said? Shrugging off his apprehension in favor of his salvation, he let it go. "Yeah. I'm sure if we go to the bedroom—"

"Why bother with the bedroom?"

He blinked. "What?"

"I can take it off right here, if you like." When did she get that sleepy look to her eyes? She never had it before. The green was smoky almost. With her cheeks flushed and her mouth all wet...damn if she didn't look like she was coming out of his bed.

"But my clothes are in the bedroom." That sentence might have sounded less stupid if he hadn't tripped over his tongue twice to say it.

"Who needs clothes?" She stood up, already reaching behind herself for her zipper.

What was going on? She was going to take off that miserable excuse for clothing. In *front* of him? "*You* do! Can't have you walking around in nothing."

She stopped moving, her whole body tensing. "Wait a minute. You want me to *change*? Into *your* clothes?"

He nodded, not altogether sure how far her zipper had descended. He only knew he didn't *want* to know. He didn't. He waited, hand extended to stop her progress, wondering what in the world had gotten into her.

"I knew it. I knew I couldn't do this. I just knew it." She released the back of her dress, bringing her hands around to her face.

The zipper made no sound of movement, so he assumed she hadn't gotten around to lowering it in the first place. Breathing a sigh of relief, he put his own hand down. "Couldn't do what?"

"Seduce you. Alice said I could and for a minute there I believed her. I mean, you had that look on your face again. I thought maybe she was onto something. God, I must be out of my mind."

Burke frowned. She was there to seduce him? Before he could make much sense of it, she turned around, still mumbling to herself, and headed into the hall, rendering him speechless. Rock hard, stupid and speechless.

The zipper made it all the way down her back. As she walked out of the living room, the gaping hole went from her shoulder blades to the small of her back without a stitch of fabric to mar the path.

She disappeared into his bedroom and he made it a point to disappear into the kitchen. Preferably into the freezer.

Chapter Six

Cass didn't know what she was going to do without a bra, but she didn't care. So what if everything swung all over the place, Hayne was right about Burke not noticing.

She dug out a T-shirt and dragged it roughly over her head. She cringed a little at the crunching sound of her hair being pulled down by the collar before deciding it didn't matter. Irritably, she undid the clasps on the stockings, rolling them down her legs as fast as she could. With a sour toss, she flung them in the direction of Burke's bed. A bit of wiggling later, the satin octopus of a garter belt was over there somewhere as well.

She grabbed another pair of Burke's sweats, this time dark blue. He never wore them, but accepted them when she gave them to him for Christmas. She should have bought them in her own size. He wouldn't have known the difference. Purely out of spite, she grabbed his favorite pair of socks—the ones with the reinforced toe and heel in dark blue—and dragged them on. A quick glance in the mirror showed her hair pretty much springing back into shape and her make-up hadn't smeared. Well, she wasn't taking that off, so he'd better get used to it.

She stomped back into the living room, finding him waiting by the window. The relief on his face was unmistakable. Cass wanted to punch him. Was her body frightening or something?

"Good, you're ready."

She crossed her arms and smirked. "For what? Wrestling?"

"Nope, dinner."

She frowned. "What does dinner have to do with this?"

"Facts are, a lady has a certain way of eating. You, on the other hand, eat like a man."

How did he get away with making his every opinion sound like a fact? "I eat like everyone else."

"Everyone else polishes off two foot-longs in ten minutes?"

She fought the urge to blush. "I don't have a lot of time when I'm out on the sites."

"Doesn't change the fact that you need a wet-nap for your entire face afterwards. Table."

She scowled as she followed his pointing finger to the dining room table where they'd played poker only a few days ago. Yanking out the chair, she dropped into it and waited for him.

"Wrong."

"What?" *What does he have to be smug about?*

"A lady doesn't yank a chair like it's the rope in a tug-o-war. She waits for her date to pull it out for her and she slowly sits."

"When was the last time a guy pulled out a chair for me?"

"When was the last time you expected it? You made me open the door for you last night. We both knew you weren't going to budge until I did."

She flicked her hand at him. "That was different. I was having fun. Besides, it was you."

"By expecting something, you changed how I treated you." He blinked as if realizing something. "You don't treat me like other men?"

Did she sense affront there? Good. It was something, at least. "No, I don't see you as a man at all. You're Burke. Rhymes with jerk, so it's easy to classify you."

He narrowed his eyes, but she refused to let him intimidate her. He could stand there and glare all he wanted. Finally, he sighed. "Just stand up and do it again. *Pretend* I'm a man, okay?"

Cass stood up, knowing she was being petulant and not caring. "Fine. You're a man. Congratulations." She extended her hand to him.

He looked at it like she was offering a snake. "What are you doing?"

"I'm a lady, you're a man. In this particular fantasy land, wouldn't you walk me to the table?"

He muttered something and walked around her to stand on her left. She started at the feel of his wide palm on the small of her back, its warmth seeping past the fabric faster than she expected. He used fingertip pressure to guide her forward, giving direction with such subtlety she didn't think to argue with it. Easing out the chair, he gestured for her to sit.

"Don't flop into it. Slide to the middle of the chair. When you're ready to sit, don't. Keep your weight on your toes and I'll push the chair up to the table for you. Otherwise it will scuff or you'll be hopping up and down. If you're wearing a dress like tonight's people won't be watching you to see how well you eat. They'll be timing how many bounces it takes for you to fall out of it."

She pursed her lips, holding herself back from saying something rude. Appropriate, but rude. Carefully, she did what he said. It was stilted, but she did it. She was proud, for all of the ten seconds between completing the maneuver and his order to do it again. By the twelfth time she sat down, she was back to being irritated.

"I think I have it now."

Burke shrugged. "What you think doesn't matter. You want me to help you because I know what men expect. I expect you to have grace in everything. Now do it again. Try to float."

Float? Like one of your lame ex-girlfriends? That gave her an idea. Straightening her spine, she went back to mimicking Marilyn. Moving her hips with a little bit of undulation, she left Burke's hand behind and made her way to the table. She would have been fine, but he never came to push the chair in. She turned behind herself to look back at him, but he covering his eyes with his hand. She sighed, stood and went back to their preset start mark near the couch.

"Never do that again." His voice grated so low she almost didn't hear him.

"Why not?"

"Just…don't, okay?"

Poor guy, he looked a little pale, actually. Finally, she realized this was getting on his nerves as much as hers. Quelling all her irritation, she reminded herself there was a lot more to a meal than walking to the table. She had better get through it.

They never did get to eat. Four hours of learning how to sit, how to hold your utensils like they were eating implements instead of weapons, proper napkin placement and how not to kick your partner under the table had a way of sucking the hunger right out of a guy.

Burke watched Cass walk out to her car muttering something about pizza. She did what he told her and kept her hips to herself during the entire lesson, thank God. It was easier teaching her proper boxing stances than it was to do this. Even now, her natural ability to physically mimic anything she saw had him feeling uncomfortable. Getting punched in the eye had to be better than the punch in the gut he got watching her wave her ass like a red flag in front of him. She managed to get lighter on her feet and he managed to keep his hand within legal limits of her spine.

The sooner this dumb bet was over, the better.

Exhausted, he turned off his lights and headed to his bedroom wanting nothing more than to drop face first onto his pillow and sleep like a brick. Which was exactly what he did.

Discovering a mouthful of lace.

Stunned, he reached out for the bedside lamp, clicked it on and stared at his pillow. Apparently, it had new friends. A little pale blue buddy made out of nothing more than every male fantasy ever had. Next to it were two hastily strewn stockings, scenting his pillow with a wisp of vanilla. When did she start smelling like vanilla instead of mud? He groaned, not daring to touch them.

Not trusting himself, he moved the entire pillow and traded it with the one from the other side of the bed. He dropped gratefully into it, barely bothering to reach up and turn out the light again. But sleep didn't come. It wouldn't. Not with that scrap of silk and lace only an arms reach away.

Burke stared up at the ceiling. He had to face facts. In two days, he had somehow developed some sort of problem. He wanted to get his friend into bed; no apologies, no remorse Hell, tonight he would have settled for the carpet. Worse, he didn't have a prayer of achieving it. Her brother would kill him and Cass would see the whole event as some sort of to-do list.

New dress, check.

New shoes, check.

Mind-blowing orgasm, check.

He smiled. *Check, check, check and check.*

The smile faded slowly. Of course that's how Cass would see it. But what would *he* think if he slept with her? Would it be a to-do list for him too? Would he merely be scratching an itch? Knowing himself as well as he did, what else could it be?

No, this would never work. Wasn't there a fable about this? Or a bumper sticker: *Friends Don't Let Friends Have Sex?* Some kind of warning to explain why *not* to tempt the big, bad wolf? Cass obviously needed a refresher and he needed a wake up call. In all the fairy tales he knew, the teases got away scot-free and the wolf ended up someone's dinner. The last thing he wanted was to be carved up by the Bishop men. He valued them—and Cass—too much for a simple roll in the hay. But mostly, he didn't want to lose her and he would if he didn't get his act together.

Hayne wasn't kidding when he said Burke was more Cass's friend than his own. They didn't get together to have beer alone, they didn't scout women together anymore and they only talked when one of them was waiting for Cass, in the casual manner of people making chit chat until the real deal came up. Burke didn't even remember the last time he talked to Eddie, a man he considered an adopted father. All the important roads in his life led to Cass, roads he couldn't afford to block.

The Halifaxes weren't what a person might call close knit. His parents retired to Florida ages ago, selling their house and leaving him as much on his own as he had always been. He sent and received a Christmas card each year, along with a short note from his mother on how retirement was treating them. He was an only child, probably why he had locked in with the Bishops in the first place. He liked having someone to talk to and a little sister who thought he was a hero. That would disappear.

His high school friends mostly had moved out of their tiny town to bigger and better things. Sel Panyon was the only one who returned and he did it only after he'd made his mark on the art world. The second he got back he found himself a wife, made himself a family and got on being the happiest man on earth. Only Cass had the kind of time to hang out with him for whatever came to mind.

He had his auto repair and custom body shop, something he was proud of, sure. But as much fun as rebuilding cars was, for the most part all he did now was watch Oprah and do paperwork. If she didn't insist on dragging him to conventions and car shows on weekends, his hands would never get any grease on them.

No, Cass the friend was far too important to risk.

He closed his eyes tightly to wipe away the ruminations, stretching out his arms to take up as much of his bed as he could, hoping that would help him sleep. No such luck. All it got him was a handful of silk.

Tiny flowers tickled his fingertips, delicate lace tried to twine itself around his wrist. Vanilla vapor drifted over him, an invitation Cass only offered because she needed a guinea pig for her burgeoning femininity.

He stuffed the contraption under his pillow and made himself ignore it. The same way he was going to ignore everything else he'd been thinking since she stood up in his tub and showed him a thing or two about women.

Cass was his friend. He was going to get her through the next two weeks if it killed him. After that, everything would go back the way it was. It had to.

Six days of movie watching, dinner trials and shoe practicing was finally taking its toll on her. She didn't want to see another chair, another fork or another pair of high heels for at least ten years. Maybe longer.

Burke was a taskmaster regularly. Now, for some reason, this project brought out the worst in him. He sniped, simmered, snapped and worse, withheld food. Tonight, he finally agreed to a "dress rehearsal", meaning she got to wear something *she* bought.

Rather than wearing anything to up his ire, she went with a long floral skirt that came to mid-calf and swished its lovely teals and pinks around her legs comfortably. Along with the matching set of pumps and regular nylons she still wore the pretty underwear Alice recommended, but she wore those as a standard now. No matter what happened with her makeover, she wasn't going back to cotton unless medically ordered to. Not when silk was this nice to her. She matched the pink fuzzy sweater to the skirt and held her hair back at the sides with barrettes. Casual, but nice.

Now if only she could get past her brother.

Grabbing her purse—Alice insisted a lady always had her purse—Cass headed down the stairs. Oddly, there wasn't any sound coming from the kitchen. Hayne usually did the cooking for the house, since no one trusted her to do it without harming something. Instead, the lights were off and there was a note on the small table atop a twenty-dollar bill.

"Order pizza for Dad?" she read, turning around and finding her father already settling down to his usual routine of the Wheel. "Where's Hayne?"

"He has a date or something. Some little girl he met at the nursery."

Cass rolled her eyes at the note, then went to the phone. Her father considered every female under fifty a little girl—except her, anyway—and Hayne picking one up at work was no big shock to either of them. Right when she was going to dial the number more familiar to her than her own, she happened to look at the card on the refrigerator. Lola's business card, with an appointment date for a root touch-up. She picked it out from under the magnet, flicking it against her nail once or twice. It wouldn't hurt to test the waters, would it? If he didn't show any signs of interest, Lola need never know. If he did…

"Hey, Dad? Do you remember Lola Velasquez?"

"Who?"

"Lola. Velasquez. She asked about you when I was getting my hair done."

"You mean the one who runs that hair place?" Good old Dad, sharp as a nub when it came to anything that didn't involve plants.

"Yeah. She seemed to think you would remember her."

He coughed. He didn't say yes or no, she should or shouldn't remember him. He just coughed.

Suspicious….

Cass stepped out of the kitchen, still holding the portable phone against her chest. "Do you?"

"Um, yeah, I…um…remember her. Why?"

"Well, I was thinking…since Hayne's going out and I'm not going to be here, why don't you call her up? See if she's doing anything."

"Because she probably is. Pretty ladies like her don't stay home on Friday nights." He fit his glasses on his nose and fussed with his chair as if it weren't already perfectly shaped to his comfort.

"They do if no one calls them," she sing-songed, waving the phone at him.

He frowned forward, concentrating too hard on the TV when his show wasn't on yet.

"She had a lot to say about you. I'm sure she'd like to hear from you."

That got his attention. He looked at her over the top of his lenses, his bushy brows forced together to form one. "She did?"

Cass nodded and held out the phone further. "She said you were romantic."

He couldn't have heard that word in more than twenty years. "I don't have her number," he mumbled. But he took the phone.

She held out the card.

"She's probably busy." He picked out the numbers slowly on the dial pad.

"Then you've got nothing to lose, right?"

He laughed, a rusty old sound that made Cass kiss his temple and give him some privacy. By the time he got to the word dinner, she was out the door.

"I thought we were going out." She was pouting.

Burke couldn't see her, placing the bowl of Fettuccine Alfredo in the center of the table next to the breadsticks, but he knew she was. Her voice had that quality to it.

"And let word get back to Luke? I don't think so. We want him as high on his horse as he can get before we knock him down." He lit the tapered candles and stood back to study the effect. He was no Martha Stewart, but it would work.

"What's in the box by the door?"

He turned around to catch her bumping the small box with the toe of her shoe. "Homework."

She looked up, her mouth quirked into an incredulous frown. "More? I barely got those movies turned back to Ernie's on time as it was."

"More. We've only got a week left and a lot left to cover."

"What else is there? We've got eating and walking down already. The clothes do the rest, don't they?"

"Not hardly. This is a wedding. It's a minefield of etiquette. Walking, sitting, eating, yes. But also conversation that doesn't involve swearing or insulting anyone. And..." He dreaded this part, "...dancing."

"Dancing?" She was right to look worried. He couldn't dance and no one had ever taught her.

"We'll have to wing it."

"Are we going to practice?"

"Unfortunately." He wore his most scuffed boots for the occasion. He only wished they were steel toe.

"Start with food, though, right?"

He shrugged. "As good a place as any, I guess."

Why wasn't he prepared for her smiles these days? The pink gloss she wore wasn't spectacular, but for some reason she lit up when she smiled. She looked pretty comfortable in skirts now. She didn't trip in her heels, which only took a few days to achieve. She still had something a little stiff to her step in them, though. As if she were a little girl playing dress up instead of a woman wearing her own clothes.

He shrugged the thought away, concentrating on more important things. He flicked the lights off over the dining room table and turned to her. "For all intents and purposes, we'll pretend this is a date. We're going out to dinner and I suppose the place has a dance floor." He gestured to the bare bit of carpet next to the front door, where she already stood.

"Will we have fake names too?"

It was hard not to be amused when her eyes danced with the reflection of the candlelight. Oh, hell, they might as well have fun with it. It might help. "Sure, you can be Gwenivere and I can be—"

"Harry."

He scrunched an eye at her. "Why do I have to be a Harry?"

The brat feigned an innocent look. "I happen to like the name Harry."

"Fine, your name is Belulah."

She gaped at him. "That sounds like a cow!"

"Good. Now, Belulah, shall we?"

She narrowed her little cat eyes at him and pursed her lips in perfect lemon-sucking form. "Sure thing, Harold."

"Harry, darlin'. Only my mother calls me Harold." He led her to the table, pleased when she flowed against him the way she was supposed to. After pushing her chair in, he took the one across from her.

Watching her between the candles, he saw her unroll her silverware and put the napkin across her lap as if she'd been doing it all her life. It was hard to admit when he was wrong, but he had to when he watched the firelight shimmer off the red waves of her hair, flicker in her eyes and brighten the soft gold of her skin. Right now, there wasn't a person on earth who could tell him she wasn't a lady.

If only he could make it last one more week and go away.

"What do you do, Belulah? If I can ask?"

She reached for the serving spoons in the salad and grinned cheekily. "Oh, is this a blind date?"

"Sure, why not?"

She tilted her head, looking up from the corners of her eyes and probably thinking up something wholly impossible. "Well, after I retired from my original profession as a much sought after brain surgeon, I thought I'd take things easy and become a rocket scientist."

"I can see how that might be relaxing. A hobby below my esteemed intelligence, I must say. I'm an inventor."

"Ooh, that's interesting. What did you invent?"

"The first pair of working X-Ray glasses, marketed for boys. I stand to make a fortune off second-graders wanting to see their teacher's underpants."

She laughed, throwing her head back with real, relaxed whimsy. Burke forgot for a moment they were playing a game. He let his gaze caress the graceful curve of her long throat, trace the line of her jaw and linger on the petal pink of her lips. She smiled at him, her eyes still glittering with giggles. When had that become more intoxicating than the wine he had yet to sip?

"When does your handy-dandy gadget hit the market?"

Burke went back to his salad. Far less interesting, but immeasurably safer. "Christmas. It's my present to the world."

"I guess my present should be lead underwear." She took a bite of lettuce. One small piece of lettuce instead of the three with a cucumber and a cherry tomato at the tip she was used to. *Good girl.*

"So, what do you do for fun, Harry?"

Burke wondered if his fictional character *could* have fun. "I make castles out of cards and read mathematical journals."

"Ah, a real wild man, huh?"

"Most definitely. What do you do, Miss Belulah?"

"For fun? Oh, I go out to the Barn Dance and pick my teeth with hay."

"I've heard square dancing can be exhausting." He watched her serve a mid-sized amount of fettuccine. Not a spill, nor was it enough to raise any eyebrows. It wouldn't fill her up, either, but she could always snack at home after the wedding.

"No, but cow-tipping sure is tiring."

Her over the top wink had him laughing into his napkin. "What do you think it says about us that we've picked probably the two most boring people on earth to portray?"

"We like to set ourselves some high standards to top in real life?" She took a bite of her pasta and refrained from the orgasmic moan she usually made with this dish. She still made the face, though. Something to work on, but hardly a crime. "This place makes delicious food. I'll have to get the name of the chef and see if he does catering."

"Throwing a party soon?" he asked, tearing off a piece of bread and lightly buttering it for her.

"Yes, as a matter of fact. A victory party. A friend is going to win a bet in a week and she's going to invite the whole town to congratulate her."

He'd have frowned, but the imp was teasing. At least, she better be. "Well, I wouldn't make any plans. You never know what might happen where bets are concerned."

"Think I'm overconfident?"

"Yes." Her face lost a little of its glow and he felt like kicking himself. "Not to say she can't win, but she needs to keep her goal in mind, not the win."

She shrugged, picking at her food, the enthusiasm she had earlier now missing. Burke ate a few more bites, none of which had the flavor of the first.

"Would you like to dance?"

Her eyes darted to his, nervousness coloring her cheeks quickly. "But we're still eating."

"People do stop eating to dance at weddings."

"Okay." She picked up her napkin, dabbed at the corners of her mouth and set it to the left of her plate. He stood and circled the table while she waited in her seat for him to offer his hand. Those movies had seriously helped; he hadn't even thought to teach her that.

She slipped her hand into his firmly. Cass didn't do things halfway, easily giving herself into his care. It was enough to make him feel proud of himself, but he wasn't particularly sure why. She would do the same if anyone else asked her to dance.

"You okay? You look ready to kill someone." Her voice interrupted thoughts he hadn't realized were black.

He nodded. "Yeah, fine, just trying to remember where I put the CD remote."

"On the table where it always is." She pointed for good measure. It was lined up next to the TV and VCR remote on the corner of the small oak coffee table. As usual.

"Thanks." What else could he say? *I'm sorry, I was mentally kicking the shit out of some guy who might ask you to dance?* She'd ask why.

A few moments later he had soft country music playing, ready to sacrifice his feet for friendship. He extended his arms, watched Cass step close to him, tentatively put her hand on his shoulder and fit her palm to his. His free hand went to her waist, right above the sloping curve of her hip where it was always supposed to go when doing this kind of thing. He firmly reminded himself it had nothing at all to do with attraction.

He just wasn't sure he believed it.

Cass stood in the last place on earth she ever imagined she could be—in Burke Halifax's arms. Her fingers itched to slide from his stiff shoulder to the dark curls at his nape. It wasn't often he dressed up, but he could steal any girl's breath when he did. Tonight, in his crisp white dress shirt and dark gray dress slacks, she wondered if he'd meant to steal hers.

The warmth of his big hand on her hip made her heartbeat do all kinds of squirrelly things, not one of which could be labeled regular. She thought the feel of his fingertips on her spine did weird things to her, but this awkward swaying they were doing with a foot and a half between them oddly was more disconcerting.

"Don't people dance closer than this?" she asked, looking down at their feet.

"Generally." *Why don't you just grunt?*

"We aren't because?"

"Safer this way." He turned her, nearly twisting her wrist in the process.

She yanked it out of his grasp before it could crack. "This isn't going to work, Burke, and it's definitely not safe."

He stopped swaying, his mouth in that hard line with the white at the corners again. "How do you want to try this?"

Good question. She closed her eyes and tried to remember exactly where arms and legs went in most of those movies. The trouble with classics was when they danced they were usually doing something complicated. She was no Cyd Charisse. She wasn't even Audrey Hepburn trying to keep up with Fred Astaire by sitting and looking cute on a chair in *Funny Face*.

Sad, since the plot wasn't far from the mess her life had become. At least Audrey had the option of becoming a famous supermodel, to say nothing of falling madly in love with the man who changed her over. If that were her own fate, she'd be falling in love with Lola Velasquez.

Smiling because she knew she was making too much fuss over a simple thing like touching, she took Burke's heavy arm and wrapped it around herself until his wide hand covered the small of her back completely. She indulged a little by letting her own hand do exactly what it wanted to his nape and pressing herself up against his broad chest. She had to bite back the delicious little moan that tried to form. He'd never let her lean her head on his chest, but oh how she wanted to. His big, warm body fit hers perfectly.

His eyes widened, which she could easily see since their faces were now only a few inches apart. Fitting her hand to his, she moved her hips back into the sway they had been doing earlier.

"There, now we'll look like everyone else on the floor."

"S-sure."

This was definitely better. She could feel each subtle movement of his hips, the shift of his legs next to hers. She didn't moan, but she did sigh. Giving in, she lay her cheek over his heart, the steady beat reassuring and strong. Telling him wouldn't be wise, but when Burke held her like this, she understood why so many women would follow wherever he went.

"I don't get why you were nervous about this. We're not maiming each other. I think we're doing pretty good actually." She breathed deep of his cologne, picking up the woodsy scent she liked best.

"Because we're not going anywhere. We're swaying."

"So move us around." She picked up her head to give him her best challenging look.

"You can't impress anyone with broken feet, Cassie."

"Come on, *Harry*, I dare you."

A flicker of indignation lit the dark blue in his gaze before his mouth quirked into a rakish grin. Before she could taunt him again, he splayed his fingers across her back and whirled them around three or four times. A breathless second later she was nearly on the floor, dipped neatly over his arm, their bodies pressed so close she could feel his lungs expand.

She looked up at him incredulously. "Well, who would have guessed Harry was a dancer?"

"Not Harry, that's for damn sure." He looked relieved, but he didn't make any move to let either of them up. In fact, he had that look on his face again. The hungry one. "When did you start wearing vanilla perfume?"

She blinked at him. She'd be confused if he wasn't holding her as if he wasn't going to let her go. "A-Alice said it fit me."

"She's right."

"I'll tell her you thought so."

"Good."

Still not getting up. Still not wanting to either. His eyes focused on her mouth. Could gazes really burn? Because his felt like it was. Her lips tingled while she waited for him to do something. Anything. Finally, oh God, finally, he moved forward.

Her heart stopped. Her eyelids lowered and she let her skin tell her when his warmth came close enough to whisper across her lips.

All her life, she thought Burke had a hard mouth. A chiseled piece of flesh, made out of stone. But it wasn't. His mouth was soft, warm and firm as it found its way over hers. She sighed, feeling the entire world shift as he increased the pressure, bettered the fit. He took that as some sort of invitation, she guessed, because he guided her mouth open and she felt the first touch of his tongue against hers.

The music faded away to nothing when he tasted her mouth as if he might hurt her. He dipped again, this time less tentatively. Deeper, laving over her own tongue, teasing her. Inviting her...

So *this* is what this kind of kiss was supposed to be like. Warm, turning your blood into honey. Cass found herself smiling into him, copying the motions of his mouth while clutching the fabric of his shirt at the shoulders.

He groaned, making her belly ripple and heat with something she'd never felt before. His hand tugged her closer still, hazily proving she was back on her own two feet. She leaned in, as he wanted, winding her arms around his neck. Closer was better. Much better.

He stopped being gentle, drinking from her mouth and making her blood rush in her ears so hard it sounded as if someone were pounding on her head.

Or was that the door?

She pulled away at the same time as Burke, staring up at him in shock.

"Hey, what are you guys doing in there?"

Chapter Seven

Burke stared into Cass's wide green eyes and swallowed. Her face was flushed, but he couldn't tell if it was from what had happened between them or from what was *about* to happen to them once Hayne figured out why his sister's make-up was smeared all over *his* face. As if slapped with cold water, Burke released his hold on Cass and took a step back.

"That wasn't us." It wasn't. They were friends. *Friends Don't Let Friends Have Sex*, dammit. "It was Harry and Belulah."

"Harry and Belulah?" Her voice, almost whispery, was flat with disbelief.

Yeah, he didn't quite buy it either. If he were honest with himself, he'd admit that a minute longer of kissing her and he would have another pair of her garters to add to his collection. But he wasn't being honest with either of them and he sure as hell wasn't going to be honest with Hayne.

"Go to the kitchen, I'll handle this."

She blinked at him as if he were speaking an alien language or something.

"Hey, come on, let me in! This isn't funny. It's cold out here!" Hayne whined, pounding again.

"Go!"

Flinching, Cass jumped and ran to the kitchen. God help him if she turned on the CD player...

Burke rubbed his cuff over his mouth, then swung open the door and found Hayne looking grumpy on the porch with an open beer in one hand and some wilted flowers in the other. His red cheeks could have been from the nippy spring night, but Burke doubted it. *Why do the Bishops get drunk and come to* my *house?*

"Took you long enough." Hayne stomped in the open doorway, shoving the crumpled violets and pink things against Burke's chest for him to catch or drop. "These are for you."

Burke closed the door, rolling his eyes. "I'm touched."

"You should be. I spent forty bucks on those flowers." Hayne dumped his sorry hide on the couch, slumping in his lambskin coat, looking more pathetic than usual.

"You own the nursery, Hayne. I think you'll live."

"Not after tonight I won't. I don't think I've ever felt so screwed over in my life."

Ahhh, another glitch in the enduring saga of Hayne Bishop's love life. Was it another waitress? Another waify girl who stole his heart as she hitchhiked her way to LA? No, this one had "damsel in distress" written all over her.

"How much are you out this time?"

"I'm not out anything but the flowers."

Hmmm, maybe not *the D.I.D. type.* "What'd she do?"

"She came into the nursery looking for flowers for a wedding. How was I supposed to know it was *her* wedding?"

Burke restrained himself from pointing out that anyone with blood in his head instead of other regions might have figured it out easily.

"She's the prettiest thing you've ever seen. Gorgeous with these blue eyes that sparkle when she laughs. Curly blonde hair and a figure that could make you *beg*, Burke, seriously."

So far, Hayne had described four of his last five girlfriends.

"Quiet like a mouse, though, and so shy it took an hour to get her to do more than whisper to me." Hayne sank back into the pillows, smiling off into nowhere.

Burke watched him sourly. *Does he play Barry Manilow in his head to match his internal flashback? Was it "Mandy" or "Copacabana"?*

"I finally talked her into going to dinner with me. I took her up to Carmel Mountain Ranch, where the nice restaurants are. There we are, halfway through the entrée when she tells me she shouldn't be there. Says her *fiancé* probably wouldn't like it."

The Copa it is. "This was the first you heard of the fiancé, I take it?"

"Well, *yeah.*" Hayne spared him a glance showing what he thought of Burke's intelligence.

"Is this the part where you make an ass out of yourself or is that still a while off?"

Hayne looked at the ground and shrugged. "No, this is the part."

At least it came quick this time. "Want another beer first?"

"Got anything harder?"

Burke would have answered, but he made the mistake of turning toward the kitchen. Cass stood there with her arms crossed under her breasts and that pouty look on her face again.

"Definitely," she said with an evil little grin.

When Burke ordered her to the kitchen, she had to admit, she was more than a little off-kilter. Stunned might be the better word. Aroused was another. But most of all, she was confused.

Harry and Belulah?

Harry and Belulah!

He had to be nuts if he thought she was going to let him get away with that one. She'd seen the look on his face. *She* was the one he was holding so tight she'd probably have marks on her back from his fingertips, not some rocket-scientist they invented off the tops of their heads. He was looking at *her* as if she were his favorite ice cream flavor. Well, until Hayne started yelling, he was.

Cass washed her face and checked herself in the silver reflection on the fridge handle while Hayne complained about his latest failed romance. Her lipstick was gone but it couldn't be helped. Burke didn't sound all too sorry for his best friend, but neither was she. There'd be another love of his life shortly. Hayne liked women too much to settle for just one.

Unlike Burke, who didn't like them enough to settle at all.

Girlfriends came and went, only mug rings are forever. Burke trusted items, not people. Even with her, he was a guarded person, only opening up about his feelings when he was begging her not to cry about something.

Or telling her to go away before her brother found out what they were doing.

Cass thought about it, remembering the hard feel of his body against hers, the flush on his cheeks, the burning in his eyes. Burke felt something more than playacting while he was kissing her. He *wanted* her.

She felt a smile start to curve her mouth. Awe made her pull her breath in slow so she wouldn't laugh out loud in glee. He wanted her. Like a man wants a woman, a *real* woman. He wanted to keep kissing her into oblivion and probably would have if Hayne's love life hadn't interrupted.

It was working!

All this girl stuff was actually working. Changing how people saw her, how people treated her. Somehow in all the tangle of clothing, underwear, make-up, hair dye and food, she had changed something.

But *what?* How? *When?*

Cass's brow furrowed. When did things change with Burke? What set it all off? She knew she wasn't imagining it. His kiss meant a lot of things had changed. The what part remained a mystery. Aside from the fake names and jokes instead of bickering, she hadn't done anything different since yesterday. How was she supposed to do it again if she didn't know what she did in the first place?

You're missing the obvious question, dufus. Do you want him? She touched her lips, her eyelids fluttering shut. Her body had yet to fully calm down and her heart still raced. Oh yes, she wanted him.

Kissing Burke wasn't anything she set out to do. If he tried to say she did, she'd remind him he was the one who started with the kissing. The hunger and power of it were nothing she expected, much less orchestrated. Cass licked her lips, still able to taste him, and a thrill went through her again. If she'd been thinking, it probably wouldn't have happened. But she hadn't. She'd been feeling. Feeling Burke, feeling how much he wanted her and responding with her own wants. Which meant…it was real.

And she wanted another one.

She took a minute pause, considering what pursuing another kiss could do to her relationship with Burke, but it was gone in an instant. Their relationship changed the moment their mouths met. Maybe even before, when she became aware of the way his touch made her tingle in the oddest places. Maybe as far back as when she asked him to make her a woman. Nothing could make any of those moments go away.

More important, she didn't want them to.

She liked Burke's confused, hungry-helpless look. Liked his hands on her, his taste, his need—and she wanted more. Kissing him was like turning a key inside her. All her awkwardness disappeared, leaving only her own desire, strong and sure. Was this how the Frog Prince felt? Tingling from the magic that made a transformation real? The same, but different in some elemental way she couldn't exactly pin down. She still had the same hands, the same body, the same mouth. But not. For the first time in her life, she felt exactly right in her skin…in his arms.

Hell if he getsto take it away before we find out what it is.

When she stepped out of the kitchen and into his conversation with her brother, Cass knew she finally moved into the next phase of her life.

There was no going back.

Why did she take down a button on her sweater?

It was still decent, of course. Only another two inches down her chest. Her brother didn't seem to notice it, but Burke did. Cass walked slowly toward the couch, doing that hip thing she promised she wouldn't do anymore, hands in her pockets and her blouse open enough to show the smallest amount of the upper slope of her breast. If a person were looking. But he wasn't. Not at all.

He tilted his head to the side.

She sat down next to Hayne. Suddenly, the room jumped five degrees, which Burke immediately attributed to his thermostat being on the fritz. It had nothing to do with the shadowy valley between her breasts now on display.

Cass nudged her brother. "Who broke your heart this time?"

"I thought you were getting the liquor," he replied bleakly.

She shrugged. "You look like you've had plenty. Besides, this was just a first date, right?"

"No." Hayne turned his head away from her. "Sally was something special."

Cass stiffened as if he'd called her a name. "You're helping *Sally* get flowers for her *wedding?*"

Hayne raised a bland eyebrow. "You know her?"

"Curly blonde hair, petite, pretty, loads of make-up and boobs so big she should wear a backbrace?"

"Uh..."

It was answer enough for Cass. "You jackass!" Before either he or Hayne knew it was coming, Cass pushed her brother off the couch, her seductress act over in an instant. "Sally is *Luke's* fiancée, you moron!"

"What?" Hayne looked to Burke for help, sprawled like an injured player signaling to the sidelines. "No one told me."

She was on her feet, pacing, her hands fisted while she tried to not kill her brother. That had to be progress. Any other time she'd be straddling him, denting a rib or two. "How could you miss it? Who else is coming from out of town to get married?"

"I don't know. If you had been working like you were supposed to, I might not have gotten in this mess. I'm the grounds man and Dad does the nursery. You handle the business end and the florals. It's like that for a reason."

"Yeah, because the two of you wouldn't know what to do with a wedding party if one landed on you. It has nothing to do with you being a brainless idiot!"

One at a time, the Bishops were nearly acceptable adults with the ability to use reason from time to time. Get them together and they turned into eight-year-olds bickering. Get either of them drunk and Burke was always the one with the hangover. He rubbed at his temples.

"Technically, Cass, a wedding party did land on him. A good one," Burke said, only half-back to his normal thought processes now that she was back to her regular self. He had a feeling it would take him a while to get all the blood back in his skull instead of places it had no right being.

"Excuse me?" She whirled on him, angry and frustrated and yelling.

Women shouldn't look that good when they're ready to kill you. Eyes bright, lips dark, cheeks flushed…his mental checklist dinged like a pinball machine racking up points. His blood headed south again in a hurry. Shaking his head to gather what few of his wits remained, Burke forced himself back on point.

"It'll look good to everyone in town if you're gracious enough to provide the flowers for this wedding. Adds to your ladylike appeal."

Hayne snickered from the floor. "If she has ladylike appeal, I have balls of solid gold."

Cass kicked her brother's legs hard enough to make him yelp. "How is that gracious? We're the only nursery in town."

"Meaning they had no choice but to come to you. Be petty and people will think you're jealous. Be professional…and you'll be the better person."

"Better is good," she muttered, sucking in her bottom lip and chewing on it.

"You want to use Sally in your stupid bet with Luke?" Hayne asked from the floor, anger threading his voice.

"She's already being used," Cass reminded him.

"Not by you. How can you be better than Luke if you're doing the same thing he is?"

Burke's head began to ache. It had to be even worse than he thought if a drunk Hayne Bishop was making logical sense.

"What do you want me to do?" Cass asked, raising her punching arm, which in turn had Hayne lurching into the couch. She harrumphed because she hadn't waved it in his direction. "Should I send her crappy arrangements out of spite? Would that be better?"

The ache in Burke's head turned to a throb.

"Refer her to someone else!" Hayne demanded.

His temples flash-pulsed with pain.

"I would, but some dumbass was so busy getting a date he booked her for next Saturday. No one could do it on such short notice!"

Burke's nerves exploded. "*Enough!*"

Silence reigned long enough for him to get a handle back on his temper, thin though it was. "I have some thinking to do. The two of you are going home. Bicker *there*."

"But—" Cass's alarm would have meant more if she wanted to pick up where they left off. But, no, he knew her too well. She was only ticked because Hayne was getting her sent home.

"No buts. No finger pointing. Both of you. Out."

He helped get Hayne off the ground and even helped stuff him into Cassie's Z. The gold and black firebird across the hood reminded him once more what was at stake besides pride. The look in her angry kitten eyes reminded him of something else he should never have lost sight of: you can take the grime off the girl, but you can't make her less a pain in your ass.

Cass lay back in her bed, not sleeping and not liking it. Hayne sacked out on the couch almost as soon as they came in the door. The house was dark and there was no sign of their father anywhere. Somehow she found it depressing that a man who hadn't had a date in a quarter-century was doing better than his supposedly energetic children. If Eddie didn't come back before dawn, she was going to be very unhappy.

Or was that jealous?

She kicked off her blankets and flipped on her stomach. Bunching her pillow under her chin, she tried to figure out what was wrong with her. For one, her skin felt...prickly. She had a restlessness that wouldn't go away and an ache in her belly. Like being hungry, but not.

Her lips were still a little sore from his kiss and she kept reliving the feel of Burke's hands on her back. If she didn't remember years of dissatisfaction with Luke, she'd think that's what this was. Then again, Luke had never once idled her needle this high and left her hanging. If she wasn't so frustrated, it would be funny that it took her twenty years to figure out the man who could get her hot like no other was the one standing right next to her.

Of course, until tonight, the thought of getting hot with her best friend was impossible. Burke never saw her that way. She couldn't be too angry at him for it. She couldn't see him that way either. Too busy telling herself he was *just* Burke. Claiming he didn't affect her the way he did all the other women they knew. Now she couldn't be so blind. Even though Burke hadn't changed, something inside *her* had. If only she knew what it was.

After the kiss, she'd felt a sense of sensual power and she'd had every intention of feeling it again. Of being desired, of being kissed within a half-inch of her panties dissolving right off her. But it faded when Hayne dropped his bomb about Sally. It refused to come back when Burke opened his door muttering for them to go home before he tied them to the back of his truck and hauled them to Luke's front yard, dropping them to wait for sunshine and utter humiliation. He had the look on his face that said he might do it too.

But *now*? Now she just felt confused again. Burke wanted her, no matter what he said. She wanted him, too. Bad. But why? She never got around to understanding while standing in front of Burke's fridge. Because he made her feel pretty, sexy and womanly? Funny, since Burke was the reason she felt sexless in the first place, but very true. Luke certainly never inspired sleeplessness. Luke hadn't inspired anything. Not now that she had something real to compare it to.

Sex with Luke was always like waiting for something amazing to happen. And waiting. And waiting. Kissing him…could she even remember when the touch of his lips excited her? How long ago had they gotten to perfunctory pecks?

When they lost their virginity, it had been in a truck bed under the stars. She'd thought it romantic at the time. Believed Luke had been thoughtful to have a mattress for them, and blankets, too. Later, she realized she'd been convenient. Another girl might have asked for a hotel room. Dinner, at the least. Not CB Bishop. No, CB was too young and unknowing, her eyes too full of stars about the boy who said he could see all these special things about her.

He used to tell her she was exactly what he wanted in a girl. She was smart and down to earth, the kind of girl a guy could talk to and hang out with. The kind who knew the important things in life and didn't ask for anything special. He used to tell her she was someone a guy could be himself with; honestly. A girl for forever.

No one knew how important those words were to her. Even now, knowing how meaningless she was to him, those sweet lies were still important. She'd never doubted her value to her family. They had to put up with her whether they wanted to or not. In Hayne's case, more often it was *not*. Eddie was a good father, supportive in his quiet way, but he didn't always know what to do with a girl, so he left her to her own devices. The only person who wanted her around no matter what, no matter when, was Burke. Everywhere else in her world, she felt out of place. Unable to belong or blend with people her age or gender. Unable to be what anyone wanted.

Some nights, long after Luke disappeared, she would lie awake trying to decide if he ever meant anything he said. In the end it didn't matter if they were lies or not. No one else ever imagined she wanted to hear them. He might never be the man she loved again, but a part of her would always remember how he'd seen something to exploit in the first place. It wasn't sexy, but until now, she'd taken what she could get.

So where does that leave me with Burke? What do I want from him? How little am I going to accept this time?

Her subconscious had no answers.

Realizing she wasn't going to get any sleep this way, she looked around for something to do and found the box of magazines Burke popped into the car window onto Hayne's lap. Nothing like homework to cloud the mind.

She got out of bed, picked up the box and brought it back to the bed. The light on, leaning against the headboard and pillows with the box between her knees, she began sorting. *Better Homes and Gardens, Redbook, Women's World...* The array of Christmas crafts and baking tips on the covers were enough to prove Burke had lost his mind. He must have because he seemed to think this was an excuse to make her cook. She wanted to be feminine. Nowhere in the definition of the word did it say "stove-slave". That's what restaurants and brothers were for.

She was about to dump the whole box when she hit on *Lissabelle*. The other magazines slid off the bed unnoticed.

The cover was gold, the blonde draped across it barely dressed and screaming sex the way only an underfed teenager can, but Cass didn't notice. Much. No, what caught her eye were the headlines: "Friends Into Lovers? Does he want you, does he want you not?", "Ten Positions to Make a Grown Man Cry!", "How to Make the First Move!"

Cass stared at the cover until her eyes hurt from not blinking. Ideas blurred her mind. Ideas Burke would hate. Ones that involved touching, caressing...sweating. Her eyes closed, her spine already arching at the thought of his hot kisses anywhere else on her body. No, *everywhere* else. His hands had textured calluses, a worker's hands like her own, but his touch sent those magic tingles in more directions than Luke's smooth fingertips ever had. What would they feel like somewhere other than her waist? A sigh crawled through her throat.

Seducing Burke made for delicious fantasies. Now more than ever she wanted to know what kind of reality it made.

But did she really want to do this? Sex was nothing to get casual about and Burke was her best friend. Sex made things complicated. People started expecting things afterward and it wasn't something a couple should go into wanting different things. Which brought her back to the original question: what did she want from him?

Answers refused to come.

It might be a moot point. Burke had all but told her sex between them would never happen. She could usually get him to do whatever she wanted, but even Burke had limits. He would never throw their relationship away for something he could get from someone else with as little effort as possible. There was a reason none of his lovers lasted longer than a fruit fly. He probably thought it was because sex wasn't important to him beyond a physical need, but she knew better. Burke never wanted to disappoint. His perfectionist streak knew no bounds and the moron feared failing. He'd fear it more if he cared about the woman he slept with, meaning he would never—as long as the sun rose in the east and set in the west—take a chance with her.

So much for seduction...

Until she saw the final cover article.

"Turning his 'Never' into 'Forever'".

She would have questioned the intelligence of thinking a magazine held all the answers to her disastrous love life, but she was too busy looking for page one-ten.

Burke woke at six a.m. as usual. If he had gotten to sleep before three he might not be so bitter about it. He hadn't been able to think straight since Cass left the night before, her expression angry, her lips pouty. If he could have thrown Hayne out and kept her there he would have, but the mere fact that he wanted to was reason enough to slam the car door on her not-supposed-to-be-sexy little face.

She gunned the motor, backing out with a roar. Knowing her, she made sure to leave enough rubber on the driveway to repave it twice. Hell hath no fury, he supposed, throwing back the blankets and trudging toward the bathroom.

"Sleeping nude these days, Burke?"

He froze. Two more steps and he'd be safely in the bathroom, able to shut the door and hide. While part of him bristled at the prospect of actually hiding from the likes of Cassandra Bishop's throaty voice, lacy garters and strawberry nipples, the rest of him ached to run those few feet as fast as possible.

"What are you doing here?"

"Enjoying the view, at the moment."

He looked over his shoulder, hoping he imagined her. No, there she was, leaning against his wall, her mouth in a curve he could only describe as lascivious and her eyes trained on his bare butt.

"I'm up here, Miss Mud Pie."

Her gaze finally flicked up to his face while her brow furrowed and her lips pursed. "What did I tell you about calling me that?"

"You don't do what I tell you, why should I do what you say?"

"For a refreshing change?"

He turned his back on her. "I'm taking a bath. I don't know what you're doing here, I don't *want* to know why you're here. When I come out, I want you back home, reading. And I want my emergency key on the table."

There, that was dismissive. Strong, not weak in the slightest. He strolled into the bathroom and closed the door, proud of himself. There wasn't a sound from the hallway, so he figured she'd take a few minutes to complain to herself before doing exactly what she'd been told. He turned on the water for the tub, letting it fill while he took care of his morning necessities. When he sat inside its dark depths, water flowed over him, soothing his aggravation instantly. He closed his eyes and sighed. Finally, some peace. No Cass, no complications. With any luck at all, a long soak would massage the tension right out of him. He leaned his head back on the padded lip of the tub, giving in to the exhaustion. A few minutes of catnap and he'd be back on his game. Just ten, maybe fifteen…

The water lapped his chest, the bathroom satisfyingly filled with steam, when he heard something suspiciously like the sound of the bathroom door opening. She couldn't give him ten minutes rest. Not even five.

"Go away." So what if he sounded frustrated? He *was* frustrated.

"You got to see me naked. Turnabout's fair play."

One of these days, she'd push him too far. Not today, but one day, and he'd have every right to throttle her. "I don't want to play fair. Get out."

"You know, Burke, I think I'm done worrying about what you want."

He snapped his head off the padding, looking over and seeing her standing in the middle of the bathroom with her arms crossed over her breasts. Convenient, because nearly every other inch of her was bared and he didn't think his control could take it if she put her arms down. Especially if she put them down to undo the ties of her nearly transparent scrap of panties.

She moved to the steps of the tub, climbing up and over as if she did it every day. Before he knew it, she was parked on his lap, hot water swirling over them but not between them. There was nothing between them but a miniscule pair of panties.

There wasn't a safe place to put his gaze. If he met her bold stare, he'd see the smoky green eyes that haunted him all night long. Her mouth had some of that shiny pink gloss that tempted him to nibble it off. If he looked straight ahead, he'd be staring at a pair of perfect, creamy handfuls. And they'd be staring back.

Predictably, his body responded, right beneath the tight curves of the ass he didn't quite remember allowing his hands to grip. She smiled down at him, pleased as punch. She rolled her hips and he knew it was over.

I'm going to hell for this, I know it.

She gasped, leaning down to whisper in his ear. "This is about what *I* want, Burke. And what I want is *you.*"

Chapter Eight

The loud splash of water overflowing the obsidian tub as he lurched forward was Burke's first clue he'd been asleep. The total lack of Cass or her transparent panties was the one that he'd been dreaming. The painful erection was unfortunate proof he was a damn mess.

Still breathing hard from his shock, Burke splashed hot water over his face and tried to snap out of it. Whatever *it* was. One thing was sure, *it* was getting out of hand. He doubted he'd be able look her in the eye next time he saw her. He *knew* he couldn't look at her anywhere else.

Frustrated, he stood up and grabbed a towel from the wall behind him. After fussing with the black terrycloth, he freed the drain and stomped out of what was supposed to be his sanctum. Come to think of it, the whole damn house was supposed to be his sanctum. Except every room was marked by Cass somehow. Thanks to the CD player, she owned his kitchen. The living areas might as well be her personal rec room. She helped him pick his couch, played poker every week on his dining room table, brought him more plants than a single man could safely explain and ate her snacks where ever the hell she pleased. She'd slept in his guest room enough times to have a side and a pillow with a dent just the size of her rock-hard head. He could even count the hallway as hers now, because it was the first place she'd ever seen him bare-assed. The only place she hadn't particularly touched was his bedroom.

He cornered into it and swore.

Cass sat at the foot of his unmade bed, her jeans clad legs crossed—elegantly?—dangling the most damning thing he'd ever seen from a manicured fingertip. One cinnamon-chocolate eyebrow arched, her glittering green eyes pinning him to his spot while her mouth twisted into a smug, plump little grin.

"And here I thought you didn't sleep in anything."

"I can explain those." *No, you can't. If you can't explain to yourself why you never gave those back, how how are you gonna explain it to her?*

"I didn't think this shade of blue was your color, Burke."

Intimidation would work. He didn't have anything else. He crossed his arms and tried to glare her down.

"To think I was almost going to do what you said. I would have, if I didn't have to return your sweats. They're in your drawer now, by the way, pressed and arranged by color, the way you like. Imagine my surprise when I looked in the mirror and, oh my stars and garters! *My* garters peeking from under your pillow."

"It's not like that. Now, if you'll excuse me—"

"Nope, don't think I will." She leaned back on her elbows, half laying across his bed, pert breasts presented like a buffet under her white, ribbed tank top. The damn girl hadn't bothered putting a bra on. Again. The other times, she'd been well covered, under some kind of man-shaped polo or sweatshirt. Even May Belle's dress left more to the imagination. This time, the dark little circles couldn't be missed. They poked the fabric up to raised little points, practically waving, and set his mouth watering.

"Get. Out."

"Nope."

"Cass—"

She stood up, strolling to him and waving her sheers like the evidence they were. "You think you can muscle out of this one, don't you? I caught you red-handed, Halifax. You've been sleeping with my stockings!"

"They were stuck between the mattress and the wall. I found them this morning on accident." A believable lie. A damn good one, actually. He'd be proud of it if he were a liar. Hell, he'd be proud if it got him out of this mess.

For a moment, she dimmed. But only a moment. "These are silk. It they were caught on the wall, there'd be a snag. There would *only* be snags."

Shit.

"I can't believe you lied to my face."

Burke couldn't believe it either. This whole mess was making him insane. "I wouldn't have to if you'd leave."

"Why are you sleeping with my underwear?"

He closed his eyes, exasperated. "I was not sleeping with your underwear. Those are stockings and a garter belt—"

"So you admit you're sleeping with them?"

"I didn't say that."

"Yes, you did. You—"

"Cass!" He roared, shutting her up instantly. He bent down, making sure to be right in her face so she couldn't misunderstand. "This conversation is over."

He was close enough to see the gold flecks at the edges of her green irises. Close enough to see her uncertainty, her worry…her resolve. Before he could pull away, she threw her arms around his neck and kissed him.

Cass's knees trembled. Her arms ached. Her lips met a solid wall of stubborn male determination. Burke stood up, taking her with him and letting her dangle rather than push her away. Okay, so *Lissabelle's* advice to *"Surprise him with extra affection first thing in the morning"* wasn't exactly solid. She would have had better luck kissing the Wooden Indian outside of Sid's Barber Shop and Tobacco.

She would have given up but—aside from her own stubbornness—she knew Burke didn't want her to. She could feel it in the rigidness of his arms. In the rigidness beneath his towel.

Pulling herself up even more, she slung her legs around his waist the way she used to force her way up trees when she was little. With the extra leverage, she was able to concentrate on kissing him into submission. Assuming, of course, it was possible.

She softened her mouth over his, gliding her lips back and forth across the unyielding flesh. A nip at his bottom lip made him start, but that was about it. Finally, she slid the tip of her tongue over her bite.

His hands clamped on her, making her gasp with triumph and relief. His mouth opened beneath hers, giving her a tantalizing taste of him as he strode forward toward the bed. It was a rough kiss, his hunger reaching out and roping her closer to him to ravage her mouth. Already his hands gripped her bottom, nearly kneading her through her jeans. Just when she was going to groan out his name, she found herself screeching it instead.

As she sailed through the air to land on his bed.

Without him.

Confused she looked up at him, ready to yell at him for screwing up a perfectly good kiss when she realized she might have bitten more than she could chew. His arms were crossed again, his eyes blazed and she had a feeling he was absolutely capable of spitting nails. His towel seemed to have run for cover as well because it was breathtakingly gone. She couldn't quite decide where to look. His face was unforgivably hard and…uh, so was everything else.

"What do you think you're doing, Cassandra?"

Her eyes flew up to his sizzling blues. *Uh-oh.* She'd raked gravel that sounded more appealing than his tone, and the look in those eyes promised total immolation if she didn't have a damn good answer for him. Still, she really should tell him about his towel. He'd just be angrier later. "Burke, your tow—"

"Why are you doing this, Cass? Everything was fine the way it was. Why are you trying to change everything that matters? Don't you realize we can't go back now?"

Back? Who wanted to go *back?* Cass didn't have any trouble knowing where to look now.

"Back to what?" If she'd spit in his face, she didn't think she could have confused him more. "You think I *want* to be the one you talk to and never see. That I *want* to be the one you feel safe with because I'm as constant as your furniture and about as interesting. I want *more* than your friendship, Burke." She didn't realize how much more she wanted until the words were out of her mouth. *Oh God, I want all of him, body and soul.*

"There isn't anything more. I don't have it to give."

"You can't actually believe that." But he did. She stared up at his flushed face, the hard edges of his cheekbones, the squared power of his jaw, and saw he did. Every inch of him marked by his control, from the slash of his dark brows and harsh line of his mouth to his clenched fists and sinewy legs braced far apart as if in battle. Why was he committed to have nothing?

"We can't change what we are to each other." His voice was low, thick with what sounded like regret.

"Last night, we changed everything. *You* changed it when you kissed me."

"I told you already, it wasn't us. It was a game."

"You think I don't know when a man wants me?"

He graced her with a sarcastic look.

If she could have reached him, she'd have smacked him. "You're a jerk."

"Better a jerk than a liar."

"I can live without that kind of honesty." Geez, why not just say he's gay, too. At least she knew what that little morsel of honesty *really* was. "Next time you want to be *honest*, you should keep your towel on."

Cass rolled over and started to climb over his mattress to leave the room, but felt his hand on her ankle, dragging her back. She looked over her shoulder at him, angry, hurt and irritated. "Let go."

"Oh no you don't. You invade my house and my privacy, piss me off and think you can run off? No way. You wanted to talk about why we can't do this? Let's talk."

"Since when do *you* want to talk about anything, Burke? Your idea of talking is to talk me out of stuff. Save yourself the trouble, you've already talked me out of this."

"Cass—"

She kicked, minimally happier when he grunted in pain, and started scrambling again. Right as she was getting to the opposite side—why did one man have such a big bed anyway?—he caught hold of her and dragged her all the way back. She would have kicked him again, but he seemed to have thought of that. Next thing she knew, he was looming above her, his body pushing her into the soft bedding.

"Get off, you big lug!" She pushed at his shoulders, getting nowhere fast. Well, actually, she managed to worm further under him as he fit himself between her legs to avoid her twisting knees. He was grumbling too, but she didn't pay much attention to what he was saying. Giving up on his shoulders, she reached up for his scattered pillows, pushing one into his face as hard as she could.

"Cass, damn it!"

"Get off." She lifted her hips hoping to toss him over, but it didn't work any better now than when she was twelve and trying to get away with his best baseball cards. Schmuck always did weigh more. He grabbed hold of the pillow and threw it across the room before catching her hands to hold them over her head. Cass was still gasping, still struggling, while he looked down at her like he could happily strangle her within an inch of her life. "Settle down!"

It occurred to her, somehow through the haze of her own temper, that he was still naked. Naked and nestled between her thighs. It must have occurred to him as well because his eyes flickered, the lines of anger disappearing while he looked down and took stock.

"Well, hell," he said, probably wondering how he got this way.

Cass linked her ankles behind his back, making him look back up at her, eyes wide with what could only be fear. She smiled.

"Yeah, Hell."

Then she raised her head and kissed him.

This is such *a bad idea.*

It was all he could think. It didn't make him get off her though. He probably could unlock her legs if he tried, but she was using such sweet pressure and it was much easier to go with it.

She wasn't wearing her vanilla scent today, but it didn't matter. He still could smell her specific, earthy Cassie scent, the one that had him bucking forward while she pressed herself against his chest. This time, he didn't fight her sudden kiss. She didn't have to press so hard, meaning he could relax and enjoy the taste of her, the feel of her from head to toe. She breathed into him, twisting to get closer, opening her mouth wide for him. Her mouth and her legs.

"Cassie," he said, letting himself shift to his elbows and free his hands. She groaned throatily when his fingers pulled her tank top free from her waistband. Small hands were soon there, pulling the fabric from his grasp before whipping it over her head.

Suddenly, there they were. Her breasts, like forbidden fruit, mere inches from his chest. Strawberries had never looked so sweet. She shifted and he couldn't help but wince.

"Cassie—"

"You can't talk me out of this any more. Don't even try."

"I'm not—"

"Good." She pulled his head down.

"*Cassie!*"

"What?" she snapped, dropping to the pillow, hair draped as wildly across his sheets as he'd fantasized.

"If we're doing this, you're getting out of those jeans."

"We'll get there," she grinned, visibly relaxing now that she knew he wasn't trying to escape. "You don't have to be in a hurry."

"Yes I do, you're chafing the hell out of me."

She tried hard not to laugh, clamping her smile between her teeth. He was having a rough time himself, especially when those kitten eyes glittered at him with familiar humor. For a moment, things were like they always were. They were in on a secret joke together; no one else in the world mattered.

Burke sobered. *What the hell are we doing? All that will be gone if we do this. Won't it?*

The smile fell from her lips, melting away until the only thing left was her vulnerability. If he had a heart it would have cracked.

"Don't look at me like that, Burke."

"Like what?"

"Like you're already regretting this."

He couldn't deny it. "What if—"

She covered his lips with her fingers. "No. No matter what happens, neither of us should regret this."

He closed his eyes. He couldn't make that kind of promise. This experience couldn't come without regrets. Good things never came without a steep price. "You don't understand, Cassie."

"You're right. I don't. Maybe I never will." Her hands slid off his shoulders and down to her own waist. She stopped looking at him, turning away as surely as she would if he slept with her. "Maybe I'll never understand why the men I want to make love to never want me enough."

God, lumped with Hanson again. And for something that wasn't even true. He wanted her too damn much.

"I kept wondering why it was never right with Luke. He always seemed satisfied, I guess. He didn't care very much whether we did anything or not. When he left that letter, I was…relieved. I'd actually started to believe—just for a little bit—that it wasn't me. But it was, wasn't it?"

He ran the backs of his fingers over her smooth cheek. "No, Cassie, it wasn't."

She looked up at him, her eyes shining and killing. "Why are you looking at me like that? Like you're going to apologize for something. Don't apologize, Burke. Tell me what I'm doing wrong."

It was the tear spilling from the corner of her eye that did him in. He tried to wipe it away with his hand but it already disappeared into the masses of red hair beneath her. "You were with the wrong man, honey. That's all."

Her soft mouth quivered. "I'm with the right one now, though, aren't I?"

Damn it all, he didn't have a choice. He lied. "Yes, Cass, you are."

❤ ❤ ❤

Cass looked into the ocean blue depths of his eyes and lost herself. She brought her hand to his cheek, wondering if he knew she could see him worrying. The rough texture of his morning stubble teased her fingers with shivers. Painstakingly, he lowered his mouth to hers.

She closed her eyes at the last moment, savoring the expression on his face for as long as she could. More than worry was there; a softness she'd never seen before was there as well.

His hands went to work on her jeans as he moved his body next to her, easing down the zipper and slipping his large hands inside. Shouldn't there have been something funny about Burke's fingers sliding around her hip to push the fabric out of the way while she toed off her shoes and socks? About the way he slid her underwear down with them, never once looking down to the animal print she had gotten such a kick out of.

The wild craziness of their earlier kisses was completely missing from this one. He was slow, torturously tender. He teased his way into her mouth, his tongue unfurling while his hands smoothed over her bare thighs. There was nothing between them now but heat, his weight a delicious seduction on her skin.

"I'm going to touch you, Cassie," he whispered at the corner of her mouth.

She nodded. What else could she do? She shivered at the slow motion of his fingertip sliding over her hip. He added a second one when he reached her ribs, trailing all the way to the point of her breast, when she heard him exhale in a whoosh. His palm closed over her, judging the weight and feel. Cass arched into the warmth of his hand, luxuriating in his rough heat. Just as she was getting used to it, he slid his hand back the way it came.

"Are you going this slow to drive me crazy?" she asked, breathless already, opening her eyes as little as she had to.

He laughed, deep in his throat, looking down at her with a smugness she wanted to pummel him for. "That was the idea."

"I don't like that idea, Halifax."

He raised an eyebrow. "Don't you?"

"No, I—" Her eyes opened wide. *The sneaky bugger.* "Do you like this idea?"

She wanted to answer him, but his fingers had slipped to the already aching part of her, touching her as if he were stroking each petal of a rose. Instead, she gasped, shocked at the slide of his fingers between her intimate folds, suddenly overwhelmed by both relief and more throbbing. Helplessly, her legs widened for him and she thought maybe she pressed closer to him, because the pressure of those touches increased. But not enough.

"You sound a little uncomfortable," he crooned next to her ear before reaching out and nipping at the lobe. "Better let me rub that for you."

And he did, his rough thumb glancing off her sharpest need, circling it and coming back for another pass. Desperate for some kind of anchor, she clung to his shoulders, squeezing shut her eyes, unsure if she wanted him to stop or continue. It didn't matter, he was going to do what he wanted.

He apparently wanted to sink one long finger deep inside her.

"Oh, Cassie…" There was no teasing in his gruff voice now; no illicit, playful lover. She jolted up against his palm, responding not only to his touch but to the outright sexual urgency in his raw whisper.

His mouth covered hers, swallowing whatever she was going to cry out. His tongue stroked hers, alternating the pace of his finger. The combination of the two stimuli had her body quaking, reaching for something too far away. He moved his kiss from her lips to her throat, still not stopping the sweet torment of that hand.

Cass didn't know what she wanted now. Her body was warm, once again the melting honey Burke took his time tasting. A kiss here, a nip there, a lick over her breastbone. Wet warmth encircled her nipple, drawing a gasp. She could feel his smile on her skin while she gripped his shoulders, his mouth drawing her deep inside. It should have hurt, but it didn't. Not when he slid his arm beneath her, pulling her up off the mattress. Not even when he stopped stroking her, instead sitting up and taking her with him. She straddled him easily, not disconcerted when she felt her own moisture in his touch.

His hands wandered her back while his mouth mapped her breasts. Cass watched him through sleepy eyes, cataloguing every sweep of his tongue, every graze of his teeth. Her own hands weren't lax, finally satisfying her urge to touch his hair. The wavy blackness felt like silk, different from the muscles like iron beneath her.

He laid her back down, this time with her head on the pillow at the top of the bed. She heard the drawer of his night table open, listened to the foil packet tear, the plastic ripple of him protecting them before he slid behind her, pressing all his heat against her, their bodies fitting like lost puzzle pieces.

Cass dazedly realized how much like a dream this felt. It couldn't be real. It must be some sort of stolen moment. Shouldn't stolen moments be at night? When you could hide things you didn't want your lover to see. She could hide nothing in the morning sunshine blossoming through the window. Then again, what was there to hide that he didn't already know?

Burke's mouth found the back of her neck, a steady, sucking kiss making her tremble even as his hand found her breast again. He rocked his hips, swaying them, timing each thrust with the pressure of his fingers. No, she would never hide from this.

Her eyes found the mirror of his vanity, the old oak frame large but not frightening. She saw her own body, flushed and shining from a sheen of sweat. Burke looked dark behind her, head bowed, his powerful forearm holding her close to him. She didn't recognize herself, that woman being made love to. Her eyes were too green, too passion-filled. Her mouth was swollen from kisses, cheeks flushed with more color than she'd ever had. Every part of her looked lush, rosy...loved.

Yes, that was it. It was the look Alice had when she was with Sel. The look her father got when he talked about her mother. That woman in the mirror was soul deep in love.

She watched Burke's hand ease from her breast to the brown curls at the apex of her thighs. Feeling exploded into her as his fingers soothed the aching there, the throbbing grew painful. Her own eyes widened in the mirror, making her realize this was no fantasy. This was her, this was Burke.

"Are you ready for me, Cassie?"

She looked at his reflection, at the blue eyes nearly black with passion, the hard corners of his cheekbones, the full slash of his mouth. He met her gaze, waiting for her answer, utterly unaware of what she could see as clearly as the daylight surrounding them. She could see his worry, his doubt. She saw everything. Just like she, he could hide nothing in that moment.

Oh Burke...you still don't know, do you? "More than I could ever tell you."

He nodded, lifting her leg just enough to guide himself to the heart of her. Slow, so slow she thought she might die from the sensations filling her, he eased his way there, making a home for himself inside her. He pulled her closer, his arm across her hips, mouth open on her shoulder. Time lost all meaning when he began to move, stretching her, gripping her without the gentleness he'd been using all this time. Now was not the time for it. Not when she was tightening, burning, needing.

Cass kept watching them in the mirror, seeing through slitted eyes as each thrust took them higher, rode them faster, making them both cry out when the passion spun out of control. Only then did she close her eyes, because she didn't need the mirror to show her anything anymore. She saw the truth, even if Burke couldn't.

That was love.

Burke lay on his side, watching Cass sleep. He pulled the sheet over them, not wanting her body to cool so much she'd wake up. He wasn't ready for her to wake up. He wasn't sure he ever would be.

What have I done?

He wiped his face with one hand, frowning deeper because her scent was still on it. He was filled with that scent, that flavor. In fact, he doubted he'd ever be free of it. He looked down at her, her beautiful face still rosy from what they had done together. What they would do again. He knew it. He needed it.

He needed *her.*

Even now he throbbed with it, hunger turning him inside-out. But so was regret. She deserved much more than he had just given her. Lust—that singularly driving force overwhelming rationale, common sense, any type of intelligence at all. A smart man would have been able to send his best friend away. A smart man would never have dared to kiss her in the first place, inviting temptation in. Of course, a smart man would never know the pleasure of being inside her willing body or the taste of someone so sweet she made the pain of regret worth it.

How long until he hurt her? How long until fulfilling her physically wasn't enough? Things had changed but good now. Like he told her, there was no going back.

She would want all those things other women wanted. Sex, of course. But she'd also want those three "T's" as well: time, trinkets and tulips. Soon enough, she'd see what he already knew too well. He was hollow inside. He could pleasure her, he could give her anything she asked, but the day she asked for some sign of his love was the day he'd destroy her. The light in her eyes this morning would dim, eventually going out entirely when it became apparent he couldn't change to suit her. Their easy friendship would disappear, lost in argument and disillusion.

Burke cursed himself a few more times, reaching out for her hair. He twined the auburn tress around his hand, the binding loose and beautiful. She looked like a sleeping goddess here, the masses of hair spread across his pillow the way it always was in his dreams.

He wondered which he would miss more. CB, with the mischievous twinkle in her eyes and a smudge of dirt on her nose, or Cass, the fiery temptress who barely wore clothes and moved like sin had been invented specifically for her. His chest tightened painfully, because he truly couldn't decide. He only knew he'd lose them both.

Suddenly desperate, he pulled the sheet away. Her eyes opened, awareness already flaring deep in those green irises. She smiled, knowing without words what he needed. He fit himself above her, closing his eyes and taking her mouth before she said anything. It wasn't enough, he knew, hearing her muffled sigh. He'd give her everything he had, but it would never be enough.

Chapter Nine

Cass stared at the dress in front of her, but she didn't see it. Her mind wasn't on rubbing Luke's face in his own stupidity. Instead, she was still walking around in a haze from her amazing morning with Burke. How had it happened? Why hadn't it happened before? When would it happen again?

Sure, he'd been a little funny afterwards. He held her close for a while, which she didn't mind at all. He kept her quiet, though, which she wasn't going to allow to worry her. Not at all. What was to worry about? Just because every time she tried to say something, he kissed her. Or he touched her. Or he made love to her again. She dozed off around ten and when she woke, he was gone. There was a note on his bedside table, telling her to come back for practice at seven.

She might have been concerned about his leaving without telling her, but she knew he had to work. He was already hours late to the garage by the time she fell asleep. Lord knew he couldn't miss a day there. The building might fall to the ground. The cars might repair themselves. The guys might fight physics to wedge into his office for an orgiastic viewing of Oprah.

People might figure out why he was late.

She tried not to think that one, but it came up every time.

"I thought you hated gathered dresses," Alice said from over her shoulder.

Cass turned around. Alice's due date passed a few days earlier with no sign of labor, and she had taken to walking in department stores to help nudge the baby into motion. Since Cass wasn't doing anything, she offered to wander with her while Sel took Reva for some "Daddy time". Alice called it "Step away from the scary mommy time".

"I do." She fingered the folds of the dress absently while Alice groaned, rubbing her belly.

"Come on, kid. It can't be that interesting in there. You don't even get cable."

Cass smiled as she turned back to the rack, but her heart wasn't in it. Confusion seemed the only thing on her mind. He *could* have called in and spent a day discovering the miracle between them, couldn't he? He could have said what she saw in his eyes, on his face, every time he kissed her. He could have done...*something.*

"You hate orange, too," Alice reminded.

Cass stuck her tongue out at her friend with a smile. "Do not." But she did. Finally noticing the hideous color, she stepped away. *Why did he leave?*

"I know I'm just the excuse here, but it might help if you talk about it," Alice said with a sigh.

Cass tried to smile. "Talk about what?"

"Whatever is bugging you. I know what I think it is—or rather who. It would sure help a lot if you'd just spit it out."

The smile wilted. "I don't know what you mean."

Alice rolled her neck and arched her back. "You're going to make me dig for it. Don't I seem busy enough? Can't you give the tired pregnant lady a break?"

"If you're busy, you don't need to be worrying about me."

The answering grumble brought Cass's smile back for all new reasons. "We both know this kid isn't coming out without a stick of dynamite going off. Might as well entertain me while she camps on my bladder. Speaking of, you better walk with me."

"Are you sure your water didn't break? This is your third trip in an hour."

"Welcome to pregnancy. Now tell me. What happened with Burke?"

Cass blushed. "It's that obvious?"

"You haven't heard a word I've said since we got here. You alternate between grinning like a loon or sighing like a Greek tragedy. If that's not a man, nothing is."

She teetered between keeping her mouth shut and spilling her guts. Both had their pitfalls. Keeping it to herself meant that she'd miss out on what might be sound, reasonable thinking. Blabbing like a deflating balloon meant sharing something personal and beautiful and having it come across all wrong.

"Was it good? Sel's been holding out on me the last few days. He thinks I might have the baby just to get back to it."

Now Cass laughed. "He can't be serious."

Alice grinned, a good and dirty one, too. "I think he's worn out and he won't admit it. Sex is supposed to help bring on labor but this kid won't budge for anything." She tapped her belly. "I can't tell you how much I miss being flexible."

"Too much info, Al."

"Then fill me in on your info. When did you and Burke finally—"

"This morning, okay? Keep your voice down." Cass sighed. *In for a penny, in for a pound.* "It was…amazing." She laughed, a shaky, embarrassed sound that didn't begin to express either feeling to its fullness. "I didn't know sex could be so…so…"

"Sounds positive. Good for you guys. I'm happy for you. You finally got it together." Alice actually did look pleased for her. Was this how women with sisters felt? Did they share these intimate kinds of discussions? Even the bad parts?

"Hate to rain on your parade, but I don't think 'together' is the word I'd use." Even Luke occasionally slapped her rump and told her he was leaving to take a shower. Burke slunk off like a thief in the night.

"Thus the sighing."

"Thus the sighing," Cass agreed. They walked into the bathroom, Alice heading for a stall while Cass stared at herself in the mirror. No wonder Alice knew what was going on. Burke might as well have spelled his name on her neck. A dark hickey peeked from the curve of her neck, disappearing into the neckline of her shirt.

Alice finished her business, washing her hands wearily. "What are you worrying about? Feelings of inadequacy? Pressure to commit? Think you made a mistake?"

Cass laughed, shaking her head. "Believe me, Burke has nothing to feel inadequate about. I never got a chance to pressure him to commit." Her tongue caught for a second at the final question.

"Mistake, then?"

Cass could only stare at her own reflection. Was that the same face she'd seen in the mirror at Burke's? The confidence wasn't there now. All she could see were doubts. Worse, they weren't hers. "Not on my part, no."

"You think he thinks he made a mistake." Alice didn't need to couch it in a question.

"I know he does."

"Men are stupid sometimes," Alice wiped her face with a wet paper towel. "They invent stuff to worry about, swear to God. Sel goes on and on about how Reva's going to eat his acrylics. Not if he keeps them out of her reach or tells her no, she won't. Not if he pulls the steps to the attic up when he's not in there, all of which he does, mind you.

But still, he's obsessed with the notion that she'll get herself into some kind of trouble he won't be able to get her out of. Maybe Burke thinks you're getting into something you shouldn't be."

"Do you think I am?"

"You're a grown woman, Cass. What does your heart tell you?"

Not much. She shrugged. Alice gestured for the door and they went back to walking. Only this time, Cass couldn't remain quiet.

"It's not like he has some sort of horrible past or mystery secret scarring him for life. Believe me, if Burke had a secret, I'd have figured it out by now. I mean, the Pope takes change better than he does. Never been able to figure out why. Maybe he has it in his head he's old or something. Set in his ways. He has hated this make over. I can't tell you how much."

"I can guess," Alice laughed. "I'd bet he likes knowing exactly what he's getting every day. Surprises are the worst thing you can do to anal-retentive types. My father's the same way. Marrying an artist went over like a lead balloon."

"Firefighting probably didn't sound real hot with him either."

Alice shook her head. "He's happy I retired. Says he spends less time in therapy these days. I imagine he'll be right back over there after handling Reva for a week." The long awaited birth of the baby would also mark Reva's first vacation with her grandparents. Another reason Alice was racking up frequent walker miles.

"He thinks he's incapable of love." Cass's spirits drooped a little further. "He says it's not in him to give."

"Is that what you want from him? Love?"

Was it? She frowned, walking out of the store and into the throng of mall walkers on the second floor of North County Mall, Alice at her side, silent. She was supposed to find something suitable for Luke's wedding on Saturday. Two days left on this stupid bet and she barely cared about it now. Her eye twitched. Okay, she still cared *some*. But she cared more about making things right with Burke. Getting him to smile at her. Having the feeling she had in his arms, in his bed. The sense she'd found exactly where she belonged. Where she always belonged.

She stopped walking, her heart doing the oddest little flutter.

"Yes. I want him to love me."

Alice made a noise of a approval. "Any idea why?"

Part of Cass wanted to shrug the question off. The rest immediately answered. *Because I love him. I'm in love with my best friend.*

What was so clear that morning had a surreal sound to it now. He'd probably explain the feeling as euphoria from the sex. Burke could logically explain anything. But he couldn't explain away this...feeling. This joy. The same topsy-turvy sensation she had when he taught her to swim—floating free without anything to support her and yet, completely in control. Would Burke smile at her with pride and triumph when she told him about this, the way he had when she proved she could swim on her own?

Mr. I-can-commit-to-a-beer-but-not-to-a-six-pack?

Not freaking likely.

Cass rubbed her face with her hand. "He's right. I really do like to make things difficult for myself." Why couldn't she fall in love with some guy desperate to find the right woman, the way Hayne was? It would be easier to fall back in puppy love with Luke and cry at his wedding, but no, she had to go and lose her soul to the one man in town who thought growing old alone wasn't a choice, but a religion.

"So what are you going to do about it?"

"Are you my conscience or my friend?"

"We could trade and you could have the baby while I go track down my buddy for some wild and woolly sex," Alice reminded. "Having been through labor, I'd recommend sticking with what you've got."

Rather than stand there and actually think about an answer, Cass went back to walking.

Alice followed with an evil snicker. "Since you are in the midst of a romantic crisis, could I recommend approaching the problem like a girl?"

Cass choked. "I don't think so."

Her friend frowned, disappointed. "Why not?"

"Because a a *girl* would probably imagine herself getting married to Prince Charming in a big fluffy dress, moving into his house and popping out some mini-replicas of himself at top speed." At Alice's raised eyebrows, Cass added, "No offense."

"None taken." Though the tone was dry.

"I got the poofy wedding dress once. Remember? Prince Charming turned out to be an ass. Burke wouldn't let me put a knickknack in his house and you know it. I don't care how cute your kids are, Hayne and my dad are children enough for me, thank you very much."

"If that's out, what are you going to do?"

The question wouldn't leave her alone. What happens now? Would they go places together? Out to movies or dine-in restaurants? What about Friday poker? Would everyone know they were a couple? *Were* they a couple?

What would happen to their relationship apart from adding sex? Would they still share dinner and complaints about their respective days? Before or after falling into bed? When she was satisfied, would she come home to her father's house to sleep in her bed by herself? For the rest of her life?

God, no.

As if she weren't pitied enough. She couldn't spend the rest of her life following Burke around, a convenient lover and town joke. Not again.

Would she move in with him? Spend night after night watching him sleep, wondering when he would grow tired of her too? She'd done it with Luke, especially in their last months together. But this relationship was different. With Burke, everything was uncertain. He was her constant. The one she could always go to. The one who made her sure about herself and her dreams. Even in this idiot bet, he'd supported her. But Burke had never been her lover. He'd never been a boyfriend. In that respect, the only thing she could count on from him was heartache, like every other woman he'd ever dated. The ones dumb enough to love him, anyway.

"What is it about men that turns normally intelligent women into complete idiots?" she asked, not expecting an answer.

"My money is on their tight asses."

Cass smiled, despite the urge to groan. "How can you be cheerful when you're ready to pop?"

"You've never seen Sel in a pair of tight jeans. A sight like that makes a woman cheerful twenty-four/seven."

"Pregnant, too."

"Why do you think I keep him under wraps?" Alice reached over to pat Cass's shoulder. "You can't get what you want from him if you don't ask for it, Cass."

"He'll turn me down." Flat. Fear made her eyes sting. All the questions she'd asked herself were just details. Tiny ones. While she had no intention of ever allowing herself to be made into a joke again, the idea of losing Burke broke her heart all by itself.

Alice nudged her hip with her belly, an accident as she tried to move in close. "When has that ever stopped you before?"

Cass stared at her. One way or another, she had to make a choice. Could she live with only friendship? Or was the love she felt for him— from him—worth fighting for?

How could Burke *not* be worth fighting for?

"Was it this hard for you and Sel?"

Alice winked. "Ruin my hard won image as a romantic sage? I think not."

"Is that a yes?"

"No, it's a 'we-had-it-worse'."

"You two are happy now. Kinda grossly happy."

"Exactly." Alice winked again.

"You know I have no idea what that wink means."

Alice laughed. "Don't worry, you will."

If only Cass could make herself feel as confident. Only one thing was sure. By the time she saw Burke again, she'd better be.

Burke sat at his desk, ignoring the television above his head. Oprah again. 'Fael was munching away on something that smelled good. He'd look, but the poor bastard would offer him some and Burke would have to utter something. He hadn't said a single word all day. It was safer that way.

The guys ribbed him, asking who he'd been out catting all night with, but they got the gist of his mood when he kicked closed his office door on the whistles and rude comments. The last thing he needed was to have them knowing he'd been with his best friend.

Of course, no one would believe him.

They hadn't seen Cass lately. They liked her—she was the only person in town as dirty-minded as they were—she was a friend. She was also a great bet. He hadn't yet mentioned to her about the pool he'd discovered his own guys were running. They'd made use of a new penboard and an old metal easel he used to use for specials. Categories ranged from whether she'd attend at all and if she'd be crying to how many punches she'd throw and whether or not she'd get into a catfight with Sally. Odds didn't exist on her success; probably because they were all comfortable with how they thought of her. Weren't they in for a surprise?

Burke sure had gotten one. She wasn't his Little Miss Mud Pie anymore. He closed his eyes, belly tightening because one thought—one damn thought of her—and he relived the feel of being inside her, holding her while she undulated beneath him, around him, above—

"You okay, *jefe?*"

Burke looked up, shocked to see 'Fael's concerned face. Damn, he was eating another one of those massive sandwiches. Why hadn't Burke stopped for a lunch of his own?

"You broke your pen." Rafael pointed to the fist Burke made on his desk. The fist now marbled with dark blue ink.

Burke swore, looking around for a rag.

"What'd she do this time?"

"Who?" Finally he found one, next to the lamp. He'd have to tell the guys not to put greasy rags near the electronics...again. He tossed the pen remnant into the trashcan beneath his desk. It missed. Swearing again, he reached for the plastic tube but couldn't grab it. Worse, it was spilling ink on his tile. Giving up, he shoved back his chair and climbed under the desk before it became an even bigger mess.

"*Como qué* who? Who else? CB. She's the only one who gets you this fired up. Remember that time she found your girlfriend's thong and—"

The loud clang of his head hitting the bottom of the metal desk drawer was probably all that saved 'Fael's ears from being singed right off by Burke's blue streak of swearing.

"*¡Hijole chingado!* Must be bad. What'd she do now? Light your kitchen on fire?"

"Shouldn't you be watching TV or something?" Burke dug himself out of the hollow under his desk, refusing to rub his stinging head.

"It's a commercial."

"Of course." Why would his luck be any different?

"The other half is over there." Rafael pointed again.

"The other half of what?" *He better mean the sandwich.*

"The pen."

Bastard. "Someone make you the broken pen police?"

"No, I thought you'd get upset if you lost it. That's the pen CB gave you for your birthday two years ago."

Burke glared at him.

The older man cackled. "She's lucky you love her, geez. Musta been *really* bad this time."

"You wanna live to see the next commercial, 'Fael?"

"Si, *jefe.*"

"Then shut up."

Blessed silence reined for all of thirty seconds.

"We're back and today's topic is Friends and Lovers—"

Rather than scream—or heaven forbid, break another pen—Burke stalked out of his office and back to the repair bay. God save the poor schmucks working for him if they said one damn word about sex, Cass, the bet or anything else. In any language.

Burke clanged into the oversize chart of bets, times and names on a metal easel two steps out of his office. "What did I tell you guys about this goddamn pool?" he roared into the suddenly silent garage.

"What's the matter, Halifax? Someone already got your slot?"

Great, exactly what I need. Feeling murderous, Burke turned away from the fallen sign to face the open bay of two cars, a truck up on the lift, a world of metal weapons and an idiot dumb enough to walk into the place he was least welcome. Luke was looking a touch less purple and a hell of a lot more smug. What could possibly be going on now?

"What are you doing in my garage?"

Luke put up his hands in mock surrender. "Just bringing your boys the money I owe them for the pool."

Burke turned to look at his traitorous employees, but they were still curiously out of sight. He returned his menace to Luke. "As you can see, no one is here to take it. Leave."

"Don't get your feathers in a twist, you already got what you wanted. I'm out of CB's life once and for all. I did what you wanted, CB's yours, free and clear."

Burke's blood pressure hitched upward. "You think I got rid of you because I wanted Cass for myself?" *How dumb can one person be?* "You were cheating on her. I got rid of you because you didn't deserve her. You *never* deserved her."

"Oh, and you do?" Luke's laughter only rubbed salt in Burke's already gaping conscience. If Luke of all people could see he wasn't worthy of Cass, how long until *Cass* figured it out? "You think she'll still see you as her hero when she finds out you're the reason she got left at the altar?"

Probably not.

"Blackmail has a way of smudging all that shining armor she sees you in. I think it's funny, is all. I mean, everyone thinks CB's helpless, but she likes to do things for herself. You could have told her about me and the girl in the hotel room. She'd have done the rest on her own."

Burke considered that option last year, but rejected it almost immediately. "You would have weaseled your way back into her good graces somehow. You always did before."

Which was why he did it. Why he'd followed Luke after spotting him in the city after the annual Concept Car Convention. Cass had bowed out, thankfully, because of bookkeeping. Seeing Luke at a cozy looking outdoor restaurant with an even cozier looking blonde when he was supposed to be in Irvine interviewing for a coaching position with a school made Burke suspicious to say the least. Enough to wait a few hours after the duo checked into a hotel room nearby before knocking on their door. It wasn't his fault the idiot answered the door in a towel while his date requested ice from the bathroom shower stall.

All of Luke's transgressions, all of Cass's hurts, reared up in his mind and that was why he took the man Cass loved and shook him like a rag doll. Because Luke betrayed her again. Because he couldn't shake Cass for staying with someone like him; for not even *seeing* what Luke really was. There was nothing more important at that moment than severing those ties between Luke and Cass, once and for all.

It hadn't been difficult to scare Luke into leaving. He loved himself and his face far too much to risk either one for Cass. No, the only trouble was not beating the whelp into an unrecognizable pulp. The next best thing to it was making him write that letter...

"I should be thanking you for what you did," Luke continued, unaware of Burke's dark thoughts.

Burke frowned at the almost genuine tone coming from the one person he thought wouldn't know the word's definition.

"Convincing me to get out of this hole was the best thing you could have done for me. I have a real future in LA. No one there knows everything about me. It's good to have a little mystery in my business. Being with Sally, well, I don't have to tell you what she's done for me. Her father is the most influential producer in film today."

So much for genuine. "You marrying her or her father?"

Luke seemed to figure out Burke wasn't interested in his bragging. But he wasn't done yet, Burke could tell.

"Don't you ever wonder?" Luke asked, his voice low as he pulled a pair of aviator's sunglasses from his breast pocket.

Bait, if he ever heard it, but since Luke came there for a reason, Burke decided to get it out of the way. "Wonder what?"

"How Cass feels about you? Let's face it, if you hadn't gotten rid of me, you'd never be with her right now. If she'd gotten rid of me, you'd know. But the way it is now," he added, "you'll never know for sure which one of us she wants most."

The truth coiled around him like a bleak fog. Truth he didn't want to hear, truth he didn't want to think about, but truth all the same.

"Get out of my garage while you can still walk upright."

Luke's star quality smile shone past the nearly faded bruises, his teeth glinting almost as bright as the mirror lenses on his glasses. The schmuck probably *would* do well in Hollywood.

"Tell your boys to pick up my money at Shaky Jakes. That's where they're moving the pool, isn't it?"

"You knew and you came by here anyway?" Burke asked, his hands tightening into fists. What he wouldn't give to bash the idiot's head in.

"You know me, always ready to chat with a friend. See you at the wedding, Halifax." A jaunty wave—*who the hell is jaunty these days?*—and Luke strolled out of the garage's open doors. Leaving Burke with just one thing to do.

"Billy!" he roared, looking around until a hat rose from behind one of the cars.

"Yeah, boss?"

"Get over here," he said, bending down to pick up the still folded easel. He scanned the pool chart, looking for the category he needed but it wasn't there. "Bring a pen."

Billy probably wouldn't move as fast if his pants were on fire. Burke had barely finished snapping when the kid arrived. Smart man. Burke scribbled a new category at the bottom of the chart, and wrote his name next to it along with a high enough dollar value that it wouldn't be missed. Billy's eyes bulged when Burke handed him back the pen.

"Now get this shit out of my garage."

A mumbled "yes sir" later and Burke once again had nothing to think about. Nothing except what he couldn't have.

Dieting was definitely out. So was dinner with Burke. Cass left a message on his machine that she wouldn't make it shortly after she gave up trying to find a dress with Alice, who didn't go into labor. Since he was still at the garage, she was spared his indignation and demands. Sadly, her stomach wasn't as gracious. It still wanted food and it wanted it now. Shoving a hat backward on her head, she tromped into Shaky Jake's and slumped into a booth. A mushroom burger and a beer and she'd be able to think.

Well, she would if it wasn't so quiet all of a sudden.

Peering out from under the light of the dangling overhead lamp, Cass realized everyone was staring at *her*. Which included the blond man in familiar jeans and jacket on the stool dead center of the bar.

Maybe it was the way he was staring at her, the way he used to, perhaps it was the full, frothy beer in his hand, but for one miniscule second, Cass remembered why she used to love Luke Hanson. The way he could command an entire room's attention, the sheer beauty of him and the way he could turn all that focus on you as if you were the only other person there with him.

But the moment passed. He shifted. He breathed. He did *something*, because all at once, Cass could see right through the illusion and couldn't find an ounce of substance behind his perfect blue eyes or artfully placed dimples. He was the same old Luke. A jerk. A pompous, narcissistic fool. A user.

No, what snapped her out of it was that there simply wasn't enough of him. His hair was too light, his eyes too clear, his shoulders too thin. He wasn't imposing. He wasn't scowling. Like a photo negative, Luke was a poor shadow of what she had come to think of as perfect for her.

He wasn't Burke.

Maybe that had doomed their relationship from the beginning. She always expected him to be something he never was. She'd tried to make him into Burke, forced him into school, and dragged him into things hoping he'd discover a responsibility he enjoyed. She'd done him as much wrong as he'd done her, only Luke had never realized it. Probably never would.

Luke's voice interrupted her epiphany. "You and Halifax gotta be the weirdest damn couple in this whole state, CB."

Cass looked up to find him lifting his beer with a fingertip hold around the rim, his weight on his back leg while he leaned down to be seen under the faux tiffany lamp's glow. *Anything to make sure those pearly whites shine.* Why hadn't she noticed this about him years ago either?

"Go away, Luke, you're blocking my view to the waiter."

"Oh, by all means," he said, acting as if he were doing her a favor and sat opposite her in the booth. "I'm not dumb enough to come between you and your dinner."

The number of things he *was* dumb enough to do made her eyes start to cross. "Don't you have a fluffy fiancée around here somewhere? Someone who actually *wants* to spend time with you?"

His eyes flickered, his grip on his beer went slack and Cass could already tell she wasn't going to get to enjoy her dinner. Too many times she'd seen this same look. Luke needed a shoulder to cry on.

"Why do you have to be that way, CB? I'm sitting here, friendly-like, and you have to go and be mean."

The fastest way past his bull was to stomp right through it. "What do you want, Luke?"

"How about a little compassion, CB. I'm heartbroken here."

Cass signaled May Belle at the bar, gesturing to her menu. May Belle nodded and tipped off a young man in a crisp, white shirt and green apron. He came, she ordered and within three minutes, there was nothing left to do but accept that her ex wasn't going to leave.

"Why should I be compassionate to you? What could possibly have happened to you in the last week and a half that could make me care about you? Did you get a paper cut? Neighbor run over your dog? Your mother started in on you about having a *real* job again?"

"I think Sally's cheating on me."

Cass snapped her jaw shut.

"Can't we talk like we used to? You know, when we were still friends?"

Cass rolled her head in a silent groan. From about six different angles, this was a bad conversation to have. "I don't think so, Luke. Your relationship with Sally has nothing to do with me."

"Who else am I going to talk to about it? Everyone and their grandmother are watching us like hawks in this place, waiting to see what will change the odds on their bets."

Cass's ears pricked. "What bets?"

Luke shrugged, tossing a thumb over his shoulder. "The one over there in the corner booth. It's a pool on who's going to win this bet at the wedding. They're guessing how many times you'll fall down as you run out the door. Even Halifax has a marker."

"Burke wouldn't bet on me like that."

Luke didn't appear to care. "It's up there, you can see for yourself. If he wins, he'll probably be able to buy himself a decent garage."

"Luke—"

"Fine," he raised his hands in surrender. "I won't talk about The Holy One."

Cass rolled her eyes at the old name.

"The point is, I can't have it going around that Sally's playing the field. Like I don't have enough humiliation in this place."

She could understand that. Sort of. "What makes you think she's cheating?"

"Well, she went out by herself, for one. She's been doing it a lot."

"You've been doing it a lot, too. Plus, weddings don't just come together on a whim, Luke. She's probably doing a lot of leg work to organize it so fast."

"I know, I know, okay? You think I don't know that?" Defensiveness. Standard Luke response to confrontation with common sense. But it didn't dissolve the lump of guilt forming in her chest because she knew Sally *was* wandering a bit. Once more, moral questions cropped up all over her mind, not the least of which was why she was sitting with Luke when she *should* be at dinner with Burke.

The kid arrived with her burger, fries and frosted glass of amber salvation. Maybe if she kept her mouth full, she wouldn't get caught saying anything she'd regret.

"Sally's different than you, CB. She wants to talk all the time, for one. The woman has never heard of silence. You used to understand things without having to be told every little detail. Remember when we used to watch football games on Sunday afternoons and be happy?"

Yup, she did. She never thought Luke put much stock into those times.

"I miss the way my life used to be."

"I don't," she said, hoping honesty might help where Luke's fantasy was running thin. "I like myself a lot better now, without everyone staring at me wondering what the town Golden Boy saw in me. Without all the knowing looks whenever you'd take off with some girl. I like being myself, not an extension of you."

Luke actually looked a little sad. "It wasn't that bad, was it?"

Cass smirked. "You miss the limelight because they worshipped you. Not everyone gets to be so lucky." She dug into the burger, watching while Luke toyed with his mug, thinking.

"You knew about the other women, didn't you?" he asked softly.

Honesty seemed to be working so far. "Yes and no. I expected it would happen eventually, I guess. I mean, everyone did. You said it yourself, I *wasn't* woman enough to hold you." It was the truth. Keeping Luke forever seemed impossible and she never even considered the possibility. Not then. She was a girl. The woman in her hadn't even started to show. "You leaving...I learned a lot about myself. Learned I didn't need to be in your shadow. I should probably thank you for going. The two of us married would have been a mistake."

It was Luke's turn to look disgusted. "Don't *thank* me, I was more than happy to stay and get married. Hallifax is the one who decided it was time for me to go."

There it was again, the twitch in her ears. "Sorry?"

Luke looked up from his glass, a very real spark of resentment in his eyes. "Sorry? *Now* you say sorry? I'm the one who got uprooted and made into a laughingstock in my own hometown. Sure, you got pitied, but that wasn't nothing new to you. *I* couldn't come home, CB. Do you know how that felt?"

She should have known all the "good times" bit was an act. "What are you talking about?"

"I'm talking about making Burke follow me that weekend I was supposed to go up to Irvine. You knew about Taimie and you sent your goon to beat me up."

Cass's eyes went wide as Luke's narrowed. "Burke beat you up?"

"Not as much as he'd have liked to. He still swears you had nothing to do with it, but I'm not stupid. I know how it happened. I mean, why else would Hallifax leave his precious garage if not to follow me? He told me to never come back or he'd finish the job and made me write that idiot letter. At the time, I figured it was better than meeting the coroner, so I did it. I never expected the two of you to hand it around town!"

Luke's voice rose enough to be heard beyond the booth. "Admit it, CB. You guys trapped me—humiliated me—so you'd have an excuse to be together without ever having to face everyone for breaking my heart. You know this town would never have forgiven you, not the way they loved me."

"Is that why you're doing this?" Cass asked, leaning forward with an angry whisper. "Dragging your fiancée to what she considers Backwoods, Indiana, so you can get payback for what has to be the most self-centered line of imaginary conspiracy ever invented? You think it matters to me if you marry her, Luke? You cheated on me and you get to feel wronged because you got caught?"

"I came back here because I want things the way they were!" he snapped, reaching with both hands to pull her face to his in a harsh kiss.

A kiss that did nothing at all but make her angry.

Batting his hands away, she pushed until he let go, snapping her head up and bumping the edge of the Tiffany lamp. "What the hell is wrong with you?" She wiped her mouth with her arm. Too late, she looked around and realized every eye was back on them.

Right where Luke wanted it to be. "CB, I know you want me back, but this is no way to go about it," he said loudly, using the back of his hand to nip the corner of his own mouth. "I'm an engaged man, honey. Let bygones be bygone."

"You unbelievable bastard," she breathed, slumping into the cushions of the booth.

Luke slid out of the bench, his voice menacingly low. "Doesn't make me a liar."

"What do you mean?"

"Ask Burke. Ask him why he made up that letter. If what he says is true, that you didn't have anything to do with it, why was he so willing to make you think you were lame enough in bed you could turn a straight man the other way. Well, unless he'd already been there with you."

She couldn't help it, her fist flew, but this time, Luke was smart enough to catch it.

"Ah-ah-ah," he tsked. "You might ruin your chances at winning the bet."

Cass ground her teeth. "Go away, Luke. Go away and leave me alone."

"Sure, honey. You should probably get used to being alone anyway, since I doubt your new boyfriend is going to be very excited to hear about you kissing me in front of everyone. Night, *Cassie*."

Cass didn't bother to look around. She didn't need to see more pitying eyes. She kept her face in her hands and hoped no one saw things the way Luke wanted them to.

But too many years of experience told her it was a futile wish.

Chapter Ten

Cass stood on Burke's porch, hand raised to knock, unable to make her fingers rap the wood. *Why all the nerves? Why the worry? This is Burke. He knows how this town works. He won't believe anyone's anxious, gossip-dripping phone call without talking to me first, right?*

She put her hand down.

Inaction didn't save her. The door opened and there he was, not in the least pleased to see her. His black brows crowded together to form his familiar, pissed-beyond-reason expression. "You plan on standing there all night?"

Impudence was the only way to handle him in this mood. "No."

"Get in here already."

Loathe to give in to any command, but not sure what kind of point she'd make by staying on the porch, she moved past him into the warmth of his house.

The table was set for their practice dinners, but he wasn't dressed up. Come to think of it, he looked almost frazzled—was that an empty cup on his coffee table? Without a coaster? She turned around to face him, questions already on her lips.

"We need to talk."

Questions died. "I can explain."

He didn't look like he believed her. His eyes had nothing in them, just a blank emptiness more chilling than his silence.

Cass slid her hands into the pockets of her jeans, studying him for some sort of clue about his mindset. He looked awful. He had a red stain on his shirt—untucked for some reason—his jeans had lost their crease and his hand looked...blue? The other was wrapped in a white towel. She frowned. "What did you do to yourself?"

He looked down at the towel before moving his hand behind his back. "Nothing."

"Is that blood?"

His blue eyes narrowed. He hated it when she got nosy. Well, too bad. She hated it when he shut her out. They were even.

"My hand is the last thing I'm thinking about right now."

She opened her mouth to begin telling him what happened at the bar, but suddenly, she couldn't think where to start. With her feelings for Luke or her feelings for *him*? Where? Her heart thumped like a hollow oil drum inside her, loud and heavy. Somehow, under his hard gaze, she felt like she was defending herself to the one person who should have understood without being told. "Who called you?"

"More like who hasn't? It's only been twenty minutes and I already had to unplug the phone or rip it out."

She nodded, staring at the toes of her work boots. It had been like that when she canceled the church for her wedding. "I didn't kiss Luke. He kissed me."

"You expect me to believe that? With *your* track record?"

She looked up sharply, the hairs on the back of her neck pricking. "Excuse me?"

If she looked angry, Burke didn't appear distressed about it. "You have all the spine of those garden slugs out there when it comes to Luke Hanson. He flicks his finger and there you are, ready to take him back no matter how it might destroy your life."

"Is that what you think of me?"

"Yes!" he snapped, stealing the tirade stirring within her in a loud crackle of sound.

"I didn't kiss him, Burke. I can't even stand him. He only wanted to set me up so you'd think I was cheating on you."

"Weren't you?"

She rolled her eyes. "Let me get this straight. You practically have to be dragged into making love to me, after which you won't even let me say good morning because you're terrified I'm going to ask you for a commitment. So terrified, I should add, you took off and left me alone to wonder what exactly happened. At what point between what happened this morning and right this second did you make any indication we were having something other than a one-night stand? Why do you get to play the jealous lover but I don't get to explain?"

"How the hell am I supposed to feel, Cass? Everyone is calling my phone telling me they saw you begging Luke to come back to you. I've seen it enough myself to know what it looks like."

"I have never begged for anything in my life." She could say that much and he was honest enough to look away when he couldn't refute her.

"You're different when it comes to Luke. You've loved him your entire life, he's all you ever wanted—"

"No, *you* are." How she found the courage to say it, she couldn't say. Every inch of her was trembling, her soul right through to her toes.

Burke stopped, frozen in mid-sentence. Then his eyes dropped. "You're confused, Cassie. Your thinking is twisting all over the place because of what happened this morning. You don't want me. Not really, not for keeps."

"Is that what you want? For keeps?"

His eyes met hers, his dark blue gaze the same she had relied on her entire life. "No."

Time stopped. Her heart stopped. The entire world stopped. *No.* So simple to say, so horrible to hear.

"Do you want me at all? Or was this morning what I think it was for you?"

"Cass, don't do this."

"Do what? Make you say things you mean? Make you admit what happened this morning should have happened a long time ago? Admit myself that Luke should never have been in my life? That it should have been you? That it was *always* you? I can do it, Burke, but I'm not the one who's too afraid to face the truth. You are."

He stiffened, a physical rippling from his face to his boots. "What truth am I afraid of, Dr. Freud?"

"You love me." He could be cruel if he wanted to, but she wouldn't let him hide. "You're scared I'm going to figure out just how much."

"Yeah, I'm shaking, Little Miss Mud Pie."

She moved over to stand in front of him. He had to look down but she stood there until he did it. "Yes, you are. You thought I'd come here and you could tell me it was over. Tell me this morning was some kind of fluke and I'd leave. That I wouldn't argue with you because we all know Burke Halifax hung the moon and the stars, so he's right about everything he says." She took a step forward.

He took a step back.

"But when Luke pulled his little stunt, suddenly you lost your grip on the situation, didn't you?" She pulled up his left hand, waving the blood spotted towel under his nose. "Tried to cook your way out of the irritation, I bet." She dropped his hand and he let it fall to his side. "Were you more concerned that I'd gone back to Luke or that he finally told me the truth about the letter you made him write?"

His color sapped completely from his face. "I can explain—"

"Are you sure?" She folded her arms over her chest. "I don't think you can, Burke. There's no way of explaining the way you cut him out of my life without explaining a hell of a lot more stuff you don't want to talk about." She waited, one eyebrow raised, for him to come up with something, anything, but he clamped his jaw tight.

"It doesn't matter. Oh, we'll talk about it someday. You can be sure of that. But what I care about right now is you and me maybe finally getting it right.

"You've got problems, I accept that. You never stayed with a woman because you thought she wouldn't like you if she knew who you really were. If she knew how much time you spent cleaning your house or taking engines apart in your head. If she knew how much you like daytime TV or how you tune her out when she's saying things you don't give a rat's ass about."

She kept after him and he kept retreating.

"I already know all about you, Burke," she said softly, knowing this was a little too much for him, but unable to hold back. "I know where you have your baseball cards and when you got them. I know how you like the bed made and what color sock you wear on Thursdays. There's nothing about you I don't know.

"I've been thinking about it all day, trying to figure out why you left like you did this morning. At first, I didn't worry about it. I thought you had to get to work. But it wouldn't go away, the thought that maybe you ran away instead. You ran away from me, from what happened, because you were terrified that I saw something I wasn't supposed to."

His back met the door. He was still quiet, still expressionless. Cass wanted to touch him, take him in her arms and tell him everything would be okay. But she also wanted to strangle him.

"I did see it. I saw that you love me, Burke."

He shook his head. "I knew you were going to take things wrong—"

She poked him in the chest with her fingernail. "I didn't take anything wrong. I know what I saw on your face. In your eyes. I know what I felt."

He wrapped his hand around her wrist. "What you felt was lust. You think you can shake your ass half-dressed around *any* man and he's not going to want you?"

"Yes."

He winced, tossing her hand away. "You know better now. There isn't a man alive who wouldn't break his own legs just to get a look at you. Including Hanson, if he knew what he was missing."

"Who wants them? I want the man who looked at me before all of this. A man who would break his legs if I needed him to. Not one who'd think it would impress me."

"Even if he didn't notice you until you changed yourself?"

Ugly truths go both ways, she supposed, but it didn't matter. She swallowed down the knot in her throat. "Even if."

"Dammit, Cassie, you're taking this too far. We had sex, I told you it was going to change things, but did you listen? No, you didn't, you never do. You jump headlong into things but I'm not going to pull you out of the deep end this time."

"You said things would change, you didn't say they would end." Great, her voice broke. *I am not going to cry, damn it.*

"I don't love you, Cass. I can't love you. I'm not made that way. I knew, I knew I was going to ruin everything if I took you, but I did it anyway." He brought his hand to her cheek, touching her so gently it hurt almost as much as his words. "I couldn't help myself."

"Because you love me."

"Because I'm a man, honey. Just a man."

She snorted, getting away from him before she gave into the earlier urge to harm him. "Didn't Charlton Heston say that in one of his movies?"

"You're not making this any easier, Cass."

She rested her hip on the back of his couch, wishing she had something to do with her hands. In all those old movies, the women had cigarette cases conveniently hidden in their bras to fondle and look sophisticated while they pretended not to feel something for the man breaking their hearts. Why the hell did modern women quit smoking?

"Should I be? You're trying to ruin the best thing to ever happen to either of us."

"I can't ruin something that doesn't exist. We're friends. Nothing else."

She nodded. "You think I'll want too much, don't you?"

"Excuse me?"

"You think I'll want marriage, kids, the whole shebang. You think I'll expect it from you because it's the next natural step to our relationship, right?"

He faltered a little. "It occurred to me," he admitted with a shrug.

"Before or after you cut your hand?"

He looked down at the towel. "Before."

"Should I ask why the other one is blue?"

"Only if you want me to hurt you."

"That one's my fault, too?"

His deep sigh was answer enough.

"You worked yourself from slight panic to a girl-sized tizzy without even talking to me about what *I* want?"

"I am *not* in a girl-sized tizzy."

She laughed at his insulted tone. "Sorry, hissy fit."

"You're walking a fine line, kid."

Cass shrugged. "So what? All I would have asked was for you to love me. Anything else we could have figured out later."

"I told you, I've always told you, I can't do it. Not even for you. My family…none of us are that way. Look at my parents if you want proof."

"I'll admit, I've met popsicles that had more warmth, but they managed to find each other. They've been happy for forty years. You'll need a better example than them."

He frowned, looking like she threw a curveball when he expected an inside speeder.

"You love me, Burke. It's only scary for a little bit. When it sinks in, you'll feel better."

"It can't sink in. There's nothing to sink into."

"Sure there is. Even *you* aren't that dense." Poor guy, he looked really lost now. She rose to her feet, knowing what she'd have to do if she planned for either of them to be happy after this night. "Deep, real deep, in that thick skull of yours is a soft spot with my name written all over it. It'll get there."

She reached up and cupped his jaw, pulling him down to press her lips to him. He was off balance enough to let her. She put all of her heart into her kiss. When he put his hands on her waist to pull her closer, she moved away. His eyes glowed with heat, his brows pulled together in bewilderment.

"You love me, Burke, and I love you too. But you were right to panic. I *will* want it all. I *deserve* it all. I want you and everything your heart has to give me. If that means a house with kids and a dog, dirt and noise,—great. If it's just us, dirt and noise, that's fine too. I don't care. All I want is you and this time, I'm not settling for second best.

"I'm not going to take the scraps you're willing to throw me. Sex doesn't interest me if it's not making love. You already taught me the difference. The decision is up to you. Call me when you come to your senses."

That said, she pulled on the door until he moved enough to let her out. She wondered how long he stood there before realizing he'd let the best thing in his life go without a fight.

What the hell *just happened?*

Burke stared at the door, waiting for Cass to come back in and explain. His day had gone steadily downhill after Luke's little visit. The guys eventually showed up, but without their incessant chatter and jokes he had nothing to do but think. Who knew how dangerous that could be?

First came the dropped tool on his foot. Wouldn't have mattered if it weren't a compression gun for removing tire bolts. Then there was the damned pool. People from all over town were coming in to place bets long after the boys moved the tally board over to Shaky Jake's. He dropped a transmission he'd been rebuilding for a 1950 Caddy, meaning he'd have to start over. The swearing only took up another ten minutes.

Thinking it'd be best to come home and prepare for tonight's practice, he got Cass's message saying she wouldn't be there. That's when he knew she was onto him, probably trying to put off the inevitable discussion about what they were supposed to do now. He'd been thinking of the positives to mention when the sex question came up—pros to maintaining it until they lost interest—when the first phone call came.

Billy wanted to make sure Burke wouldn't kill him if they changed the odds on the pool. Next came May Belle, wanting to cushion the blow. Then Old Ben Friedly muttering something about fickle women and lost opportunities. The next two got his answering machine. He made it a point to carefully remove the cord from the wall so he wouldn't find himself ripping out the plaster while giving the wire a satisfying yank.

The thought of Cass and Luke, back together... His chest had tightened painfully, his head threatened to implode and his teeth ground a half-inch down. There was simply no rest for his mind. He tried to cook and damn near took a finger off.

It was a hell of a time for Cass to come waltzing in to tell him he was in love with her.

Now, he sat on his couch, holding his finger tight in a towel and wondering how well he knew his best friend. Hell, how well did he know *himself?*

Cass always was too big for her britches, but he also always knew she was just a scared little girl under all her bravado. He had hoped when she finally fell in love with someone, it would be with a man who was careful with her heart, someone who could give her everything she deserved. The house, the kids, the dog she mentioned. It was disappointing as hell when he thought that man was Luke Hanson. But at least there was always a chance Luke could grow a brain and a set of balls. Medical science advanced more every day. When the relationship ended, he'd renewed his hopes she'd find someone worthy of her. It was never supposed to be him.

He stared at the door a while longer.

What were they supposed to do now that it was?

Cass pulled up to the front of her house, not sure exactly how she felt. Either she'd done something amazing or incredibly stupid. Rather than smack her head on the steering wheel until she lost consciousness, she got out and crossed the lawn to the house. She heard the music right before she reached the door. Loud, melodic music. *Dean Martin?*

She turned the knob and stepped into the foyer, immediately stunned by not only the sound of music but of laughter.

"Dad?" She closed the door, wandering toward the lit kitchen and stared, awe-struck, at the most unlikely sight imaginable. "*Lola?*"

The couple stopped mid-dance step, Lola dipped until her stiff hair was nearly touching the ground. She waved with the hand that should have been on Eddie's shoulder. Cass wondered if the color in her cheeks was from the pull of gravity or something a little more…exciting. She guessed the latter because Eddie had a matching shade to his cheekbones.

If her own love life didn't suck lemons, this would be a good thing.

Eddie picked Lola up and steadied her with a hand to her back before reaching for the stereo remote on the kitchen table and abruptly cutting the music. "Lola was reminding me how to tango."

Since when did he know *how to tango?*

"Yes, your father is still a wonderful dancer." Lola kissed Eddie's cheek while patting the other one with her hand. Cass watched him turn two shades redder. "We'll go dancing tomorrow, Eddie. I know a great place, you'll love it. Bye everyone!" Grabbing her purse, Lola sashayed back the way Cass just came.

"Wait, I'll walk you out!" Eddie hurried to follow her, brushing past Cass with…impatience?

"Oh, Eddie, you're such a gentleman!" The giggles echoed until the door closed firmly behind them.

"Gross, isn't it?"

Cass spun around, surprised to see her brother sitting on the stairs, a beer dangling from the hand resting on his knee.

"It's…uh…well, I don't know if I'd say gross—"

"It's weird is what it is. He didn't even turn on the Wheel." A first in about ten years. "Aren't you supposed to be practicing with Burke?" Hayne eyed her suspiciously as he took a swig off the bottle.

"We canceled for tonight. He had some other plans." With nothing else to do, she decided to go up to her room. Too bad Hayne took up all the space on the steps.

"He have a date or something?"

"No, he did not have a date." She tried the right side of him.

He slumped that way, his eyes narrowing on her. "What's on your neck?"

She froze. "I don't have anything on my neck." Thinking she'd better get out of there before Hayne remembered what addition was, she moved left.

He followed her, his beer hand dropping slightly. "Yes, you do. It looks like a bruise—"

One...

"If I didn't know better—"

Plus...

"But who'd give you one of those—?"

One...

Cass feinted right just as Hayne hit the equal sign.

"Holy—"

Taking advantage of his shock, she leapt to get past him, only to be caught on his arm and suspended midair with a scream as he lifted her onto his shoulder in a fireman's carry. "First beer, huh?" she asked, dangling over his back.

"Last one, too." He punctuated the sentiment by smacking the flat of his hand on her backside hard enough to echo in the living room.

She tried to kick, yelling for him to put her down, but he had enough practice at this to bind her at the calves. Angry and without options, she reached down into the back of his jeans and yanked the elastic of his BVDs hard enough to give him a rug burn he'd feel for the next two weeks. He screeched and dumped her over the arm of the couch. Cass flipped on her stomach and watched him swear while doing a dance that reminded her of the neighbor's dog after the last chili festival.

"Sonuvabitch, CB!"

"You asked for it, and I told you not to call me that anymore!"

"You're my dumb sister, I'll call you anything I want. Damn, did you have to pull 'em so high?"

Cass stood on her knees in the middle of the couch and crossed her arms. He might be whining, but he did still have the stairs blocked, the schmuck. "I'm not a sack of potatoes, you know. You can't pick me up and throw me around anymore."

"Like you don't give as good as you get," he grumbled, shifting his hips and trying to right his pants.

The front door opened, revealing the unusual sight of Eddie Bishop looking upset? Behind him, Lola waved. At least, Cass figured it was Lola. Why hadn't she ever noticed how tiny the woman was? You could only see her hand from behind Eddie's big frame.

"Did the two of you notice we had company? People can hear you screaming all the way down the block!"

Cass looked over at Hayne. Was her father actually scolding them?

"She was the one screaming."

She crossed her arms and rolled her eyes. "Like he can't tell you scream in a higher pitch than me?"

"Well, at least I don't have a hickey the size of Texas on my neck!"

"At least *I* don't have my hands halfway up my butt looking for the hem of my underwear!"

"I wouldn't be looking for my underwear if *you* didn't sleep with *Burke!*"

Cass opened her mouth to say something, but nothing could quite come out. Even Hayne seemed to have sensed he'd gone too far because he turned a subtle shade of red that had nothing to do with his condition.

"Are you two done?" Eddie asked, pulling Lola around himself so he could close the wide open door. The door leading to the echoing walk-up, that led to the cul-de-sac carved into a hill that amplified every sound on the block. The block of noisy people who were most likely already on their phones chit-chatting about this newest wrinkle in the debacle known as Cass Bishop's life.

"I swear, the two of you are as bad as third graders. You," Eddie growled, pointing at Hayne. "If you're so mad about that girl not breaking up with her boyfriend, quit trying to date engaged women. And stop being jealous that your sister's having sex when you aren't. You," he knocked none too lightly on Cass's head, "you getting married?"

Cass lifted her head, spitting her hair out of her mouth. "Like I know anymore."

"Good enough. You get that straightened out with Burke, 'bout time the two of you did something interesting. I was bored waiting for you. Now, Lola and I are going out for some peace and quiet. Don't wait up." He grabbed his coat while Lola shimmied over in her heels and fluffed Cass's hair over the back of the couch.

"Never let them see you with flat hair, *chulita*." Lola kissed her cheek, whispering in her ear. "He told me you said to call me. *¡Gracias, mija! I owe you big!* You have a dress for the wedding yet?"

Cass groaned, but Lola just nodded. "May Belle didn't think so. You're tall like her, she'll have something special. I'll tell her to send it over. Come over Saturday at eight! I'll fix you up good!" she called, following Eddie out the front door, her wooden heels clonking on the foyer tiles.

Cass and Hayne stayed in their places for a few silent moments after the door clicked shut.

"Am I the only one who thinks the body snatchers visited our house?"

"You're still the same, aren't you?" she grumbled.

"Why mess with perfection?"

Snorting her opinion of that comment, Cass got off the couch and headed for the stairs.

"You really think you're gonna marry Burke?"

If he didn't sound genuinely worried, Cass would have ignored him. Instead, she got to the next level and turned to shrug. "He loves me. He'd be making the biggest mistake of his life if he didn't want me."

He looked like he was trying to soften some bad news. "Burke won't settle down with anyone, Cass. It's not in him."

"Yes, it is. He just doesn't know it." She had to believe. Her entire future hinged on it. "I'll find a way to make him see."

Hayne's expression turned thoughtful. "I can believe Burke loves you, Cass. I mean, I've seen him with you all our lives. Why do you think I kidded him about keeping his hands off you? But what if love isn't enough? What if how you feel can't change the way things are?"

"Then you *do* something. Anything. You don't sit there and wait for happiness to fall in your lap. Look how long Dad sat there. One phone call later and he's tangoing in the kitchen." And yelling at his kids, but they had that coming.

Hayne hitched a shoulder. "What's your plan with Burke?"

All her fervor disappeared, replaced by indecision. "I...I don't know."

He slid his hands into his jeans pockets. "I guess if anyone has a shot at changing his mind, it's you. You two would even be good for each other. He's the only one who can make you see reason and you're the only one to ever make him stop seeing it. But—"

"But what?" she asked, somewhat touched by his comment.

"I don't want you to get hurt again. Last time…" His face got the angry-lost look usually reserved for women he wanted to save. He'd never directed any of his protective urges to her before. Or maybe she never gave him enough credit. "I don't think any of us could watch you get hurt like that again, Cassie."

She smiled at him. When he wasn't an idiot jerk, Hayne was a pretty good brother. "I'm not going to. Honest. I finally have what I want in my sights and I plan to get it."

"Burke?"

"Nope. Myself." She didn't bother to explain it to him, instead waving him off. "Night, Hayne."

"Cassandra!"

The bellowing made Cass lift her face off her pillow a good six inches before she even considered opening her eyes. Swiping at a magazine adhered to her face, she rubbed her cheek to wake it up.

"Cass, get your tail down here!" A few dates with Lola and suddenly the lump of humanity on the recliner had a personality?

Bleary, she rolled out of her bed in her sleep boxers and shapeless T-shirt, dragging her feet to her bedroom door. "Dad?"

Moving down the steps, she saw him frowning down at the kitchen table. He pointed to a sheet of paper on the surface. "Do you know what this is supposed to mean?"

Uh-oh. It was one of those moments when you knew everything was about to blow up in your face. As usual, it had Hayne's handwriting all over it. Cass made herself go to the table and pick up the paper.

Dad and Cass,

Have to make some arrangements. I'll be gone for a few weeks. I have to try one more time. Wish me luck and don't let Cass burn my pots.

—Hayne

"What damn fool thing is he up to now?"

Cass stared up at her father. "I don't know. This is news to me." She frowned. "Since when do you pay attention to his other damn fool things?"

Eddie made a rude noise. "You think just because I ignore your arguments I can't hear you? The TV only gets so loud, Cass."

Good point. "You never cared before."

"The two of you never quit working before. Which reminds me, you'll have to cover for him."

Cass's jaw dropped. "I'm on vacation until Monday!"

"Not anymore. Get changed, I'll be in the truck in five minutes."

"But Dad—"

"Changed, CB. Now."

She considered putting up an argument, but the look on his face showed her she'd get nowhere. Quick. Stomping up the steps, she vowed then and there to kill her brother the next time she got her hands on him.

Chapter Eleven

Cass griped to herself in the back of the nursery, clearing her floral section and wondering how Hayne could make such a mess in less than two weeks. Her orders were everywhere, dates hastily scribbled, names nearly illegible. She added the crimes to his ever-growing list as she swept spilled dirt from behind her counter.

"Excuse me, is Hayne Bishop on today?"

She spun around at the barely whispered question, nearly dropping her broom. *"Sally?"*

The diminutive blonde took a step back, nearly tripping on her stilts. "You! Oh, please don't hit me!"

Cass would have been offended but, well, it *was* the only thing Sally had ever seen her do. "I'm not going to hit you."

Sally, blue doe-eyes wide, gripped her little clutch purse in front of her like it contained government secrets. Her cloud of blonde hair trembled with her as she pressed her perfectly glossed pink lips together. "You sure?"

Cass put her hands flat on the counter as a show of faith. "Positive. What can I do for you?"

"Oh, nothing. It's okay—"

"I thought you were looking for Hayne." Okay, for that, Cass could hit her. Hayne actually did seem abnormally heartbroken. On the other hand, Sally didn't look too good either. Her color was off. Maybe her make-up wasn't quite right? Funny, Cass wouldn't have even noticed two weeks ago, but now... Now she could see the worry puckering Sally's brow as she looked around to see if anyone heard Cass mention her brother's name. Hurrying up to the counter, Sally gazed up desperately. *Geez, you'd think she was on the run or something.*

"You have to tell him I'm sorry. I didn't...I never meant..." Tears filled her eyes and Cass realized her brother never had a prayer—blonde, desperate for a hero and marrying the wrong guy. Oh, yeah, not a chance in Hell. "He wasn't supposed to get hurt."

Cass crossed her arms, determined not to be moved. Unlike the men in this town, tearful blue eyes and boobs about to spill out of matching blue dresses had no effect on her. "Well, he did."

Sally made a little sound of pain. Not a sigh, not a sob, something in between. "I told him my plans were already made. I'd made a commitment. He wanted to spend time with me anyway. Can you imagine that? He said he'd take whatever memories we could make before he lost me forever."

Cass was kind of glad that Sally was marrying Luke. Hayne would have snapped her up in two seconds flat, and God only knew what kind of kids they'd have. Some frightening, over-emotional cross between William Shatner and Engelbert Humperdink, no doubt.

"It wasn't right, I know, but...I've never known anyone like your brother. He's honest."

"Uh-huh." Cass felt her conscience twitch a little when Sally's heart shaped face flushed and her eyes went dreamy.

"He listens to what I think. No one else ever has. He's so easy to talk to. He didn't laugh at all my dreams like everyone else. He treats me like I'm real instead of some doll, you know?

"All my life, I've been something to show off for my father, even for Luke. But Hayne didn't care if my make-up was perfect or if I wanted to wear house slippers instead of these things." She wiggled her dark blue shoes. "You know what I mean, the way Luke makes us dress up all the time," she added as if commiserating.

Cass laughed, she couldn't help herself. "Luke didn't make me do anything. I doubt he even noticed I was there at the end."

The dreamy look erased, becoming consternation. "But you're all Luke has ever talked about. From the first time we met, he's talked about you. You're the love of his life."

Cass leaned forward. "Are you drunk?"

Sally straightened with a pout. "Why do people keep asking me that?"

Cass left that one alone. "Go back to Luke talking about me. Why did he say?"

"He said he always felt bad about breaking your heart the way he did. Said you deserved better than him. When we first met he was heartbroken. He said he made a mistake and wanted to come home and make it up to you but it was too late, so he started over in Hollywood. He was so upset when he found out you were seeing that guy, Burke. That's when he said we should do the wedding now. If he was able to get married in front of you, he could finally close this chapter of his life."

Cass felt a ripple of...what was that? Apprehension? No, suspicion. "He told you he was heartbroken over me when he first met you?"

Sally nodded. Cass swore. *That lousy, pesky, sniveling...* She worked to come up with a good enough insult. Nothing was quite low enough.

Cass rubbed her eyes with the back of her arm. Luke's infamous pity date. He used it with good success back in high school, going from girlfriend to girlfriend, "heartbreak" to "heartbreak". Always she was the cause. No one ever understood how someone like her could break Luke's heart, but there wasn't a girl in Rancho Del Cielo who didn't take the opportunity to comfort him when she had it.

Sally looked a little too nice to be stuck with the likes of Luke Hanson—galling as it was to admit—but Cass considered the wisdom of being the reason Sally dumped Luke like a piece of soggy bread. Her brother was already the reason Sally was cheating.

"Never mind," Cass said, expelling a breath. *Do not get involved.* "You want me to try to get word to Hayne? I don't know where he went, but—"

"He left?"

Cass caught herself at the utter desolation in Sally's voice. She nodded. *Don't get involved—much.* "Last night."

"Oh."

Why did that sound make Cass feel like she'd stolen the ruby slippers off Dorothy's feet and tried to stomp her dog? *Don't get...ah hell.* "Do you want me to give him a message?"

"Yeah, tell him I..." Sally's mouth hung open until she closed it, carefully, a few moments later. "No, no message. I...I have to go. I'll see you at the wedding tomorrow." She turned to leave.

"Sally," Cass called out, unable to help herself. After all, no one deserved to marry Luke. "Are you sure you still want to go through with this?"

Sally's smile was sad, something you wouldn't expect from someone so perky. "It sure seemed like a good idea when he asked me." She waved hastily and left, her shoes clicking on the concrete walkway.

It took Cass a few minutes to get over her niggling conscience and head into the back room where Hayne was supposed to have set up the flowers for tomorrow's wedding. No doubt it would be a mess of untold proportions.

Except it wasn't.

She stared in awe at the twelve basket-stand arrangements, perfectly arranged into works of art. Bouquets were set, beribboned beautifully, alongside boutonnières that could have been die-cut. Cass stayed there for a long time, staring at those flowers and wondering if there was any way at all tomorrow wouldn't be a disaster, even if the wedding went off without a hitch.

Especially then.

Burke sat on the edge of his bed, watching the sun come up while sipping coffee. He hadn't gotten much sleep, but he'd done quite a bit of thinking. Considering how much he did regularly, that was saying something. In the end, he came to a conclusion he didn't want to be having.

He was a shallow man.

He'd never harbored the delusion he was a nice man or even a pleasant one, but he did like to imagine he was a decent one with a modicum of depth. But he wasn't. He was as superficial as the next guy. Just as idiotic, too.

For twenty-some years, he'd managed to overlook the most amazing woman he'd ever have the privilege of knowing. Sure, he'd gotten to know everything there was to know about her, but he hadn't *seen* her. Not the way she should have been seen. No, he had to wait until she was buck-naked in his bathroom. Until she was a butterfly escaping her cocoon. Of course, by then, he was the jerk trying to stuff her back in; afraid this massive change in her would change everything.

But dyeing her hair hadn't changed the elements of Cassandra Bishop. Elements he finally realized why he hadn't taken any deeper looks at over the years. If he had, he'd have known long ago that she owned him.

He mulled over Cass's plan to become someone else most of the night, still wondering why she couldn't be happy with what she was. That had stuck in his craw the most. He knew well and good she had every right to change things about herself, knew part of his irritation had to do with his utter distaste for change. Most of it, really. You could never change just one thing and if you were dumb enough to think you could, you learned the hard way that things would never be the same again. Of course Cass didn't listen to his warnings. Cass never did.

Which was how it happened.

That one thought made everything click into place, almost audibly snapping together. No matter what she did to herself, he finally realized, she hadn't changed at all. She still had the same smile, the same skin, the same laugh. The devilish glint in her eyes hadn't gone anywhere. She still argued without logic and wrestled like a wildcat. All she had done was start showing parts of herself he hadn't seen before. Her legs, her figure, her sensuality, her femininity.

Her heart.

And it was his.

It was about three a.m. when he remembered what she said about Luke never being the right one in her life. That it should have been him. It was always him. She didn't love Luke. She never loved Luke.

She loved *him*. Somehow, some miraculous way, Cass loved him, perks, quirks and all. Sleep refused to come after his epiphany. Peace even more elusive. The truth chanted constantly until he accepted the next logical part of the equation. He loved her, too.

It took a while to sink in, as she said it would. He stared up at the ceiling, seeing only the many phases he'd seen her through in her life. Every smile, every wink, every laugh…they were all special to him. Precious. Even the tears she cried for another man, because she came to *him* to cry them. How many times had he ever laughed without her?

How often did he enjoy anything unless he was imagining what she would think of it?

Had he ever *not* loved her?

It explained so much. Things he'd rather not have admitted. That he was a jealous ass. An unforgivable schmuck. He'd even managed to make her think it took her makeover to make her attractive to him and still she loved him.

He didn't deserve her—about the only part of his thinking these last two weeks that was spot on—but he wanted her. He needed her. He loved her, and damn it, they belonged together. Finally at dawn, he walked into his bathroom and began to plan how to make it all up to her.

First, he'd let her get through the wedding from hell. Let her show the entire town what they had been missing and skipping. Watch her make Luke Hanson swallow his own tongue, turn every head in town so they could finally see what even he had ignored far too long.

Then he'd make his move.

Saturday morning. The sun shone, the birds sang and the church filled to overflowing. In more ways than one.

"Should you be here?" Burke asked the blonde next to him. She was squinting one eye and holding the back of the pew in front of them with a grip guaranteed to rip the wood apart.

"Oh sure," she huffed, not in the least reassuring.

"Alice…most people go to the hospital when they're in labor."

She shuddered a little, releasing a breath before shocking the hell out of him by smiling. "It took me eighteen hours to have Reva and this one hasn't even broken her water. Trust me, I'm fine."

"Should you be in pain this early?" He eyed her nervously. So far nothing had burst out of her chest or anywhere else.

She shrugged. "This kid is a week overdue. There's no such thing as early. Got any crackers? I'm hungry."

Burke tried to look around her to her husband on her other side, but it wasn't so easy. "Are you timing these things?"

Sel leaned as far forward as he could. "They're eight minutes apart. She's right, we have plenty of time before Junior makes his appearance."

"*Her* appearance," Alice corrected.

"No, you won the coin toss on the last kid. I get to pick this one." Sel patted Alice's black-silk covered belly affectionately. She smiled back, her hand still rubbing her protruding belly on the other side. "Besides, there's no way we were going to miss seeing this disaster."

"You two are sick." Burke ran his hand through his hair, telling himself he wasn't nervous. Just because the wedding was supposed to start in five minutes and Cass still wasn't here.

"No, we got fifty bucks on it in the bar pool. We wanna see our money quadruple." Sel laughed, making Burke turn back to him in surprise.

Alice started hee-heeing again, this time her stomach rippling visibly under the silk. "Whoa, she's not liking these," she muttered to no one in particular.

"That wasn't eight minutes, Sel." Burke tried to quell the panic rising inside. He was still wrapping his head around love. He was *not* prepared for birth.

The couple ignored him. Sel put an arm around his wife, whispering something in her ear while they both stared at his watch. For being in the middle of a church while most of the town milled around them, it was remarkably intimate.

Well, until Alice let loose a wail of pain he never would have imagined coming from the former firefighter. Then *everyone* turned to look at them and intimacy was the last thing to worry about.

"I'd say that's a clue to get out of here," Sel said with a chuckle, despite his face being etched with concern. "Can you stand?"

"No. I'm here for the duration," she said through her teeth. "I think the baby just put this delivery on fast forward."

"They can do that?" Burke asked, shocked into standing up.

"She can do whatever the hell she wants. Oh, *God!*" Alice rocked forward, her face turning red with exertion.

"Angel, we gotta get you out of here—"

"Hey!"

Burke spun around to find a somewhat less bruised Luke Hanson standing behind him in a tuxedo with blotchy cheeks most likely not brought on by joy for the happy event trying to take place. "You can't have that baby here! I'm about to get married!"

Alice and Sel looked up with wide eyes. Alice's narrowed.

Burke's closed. This could get ugly.

"It's not like I can stop it, Luke," she said through gritting teeth.

"You can get up and go to the hospital like any sane person would." Luke's attempt at a stage whisper was at least appropriate. The entire town *was* watching him make an ass out of himself.

"Oh, yeah, I'd like to see you pick up forty pounds of baby and water while *your* body tries to turn itself into a pretzel!"

"Look," Burke interrupted. It was only the matter of another exchange before Sel got into it and it probably wasn't a good idea to get arrested for murder the same day your baby is born. "Luke, you get someone to call nine-one-one. Sel, you and I are going to carry Alice into the pastor's office where she can lay down. Does that sound amenable to everyone?" He didn't wait for the grumbles to become affirmative. "Good. Alice, let's see if we can get you on your feet, okay?"

She nodded, something for which Burke decided to be eternally grateful. Taking her hand while Sel reinforced her from behind, they got her up. A few steps to the side and they'd be able to whisk her out with hardly any more of a scene. Finally moving past the end of the pew, Alice smiled at Burke with a bit of pride. Maybe those contractions had settled a little.

"Uh-oh," she said, before nearly breaking his hand—probably Sel's, too—and shuddering with another contraction. This time, however, the shout of agony wasn't hers. Neither was the swearing.

"My shoes! Oh my God, she peed on my shoes!" Luke yelled, stepping back from the puddle that had burst from her.

"Her water broke, you idiot," came a crotchety old female voice from the crowd. Laughter rippled through the church.

"Oops," Alice said breathlessly, a sheen of moisture shining on her face. Funny, but until that moment Burke never realized how pretty she was.

"Let's get you somewhere you can relax, angel." Sel lifted her while Burke cleared people away and led them to the office behind the pulpit. There was a couch in there where she could wait for the paramedics. Burke only hoped it was soundproof.

He closed the door and was all set to go back to his seat when he finally saw what he was waiting for, bringing his heart to a thudding stop.

She stood right inside the church double doors looking like something out of an Audrey Hepburn film. From somewhere she had gotten a wide-brim white hat that tilted over one eye, her auburn hair pulled tight and tucked into it. The black edge of the brim blended with the oversize opaque sunglasses. All he could see of her face was her perfect skin and the rich red of her lips. It was all he needed to breathe easy.

Not that the rest wasn't a treat.

The dress should have been outlawed, but managed to be classy. Or maybe it was her. White, with thin straps, it fit over every curve like it was painted on. Heart shaped over her breasts, it revealed enough sun-kissed skin to make every man in the building race for a confessional. Her waist looked tiny, circled by a thick, patent-leather belt—black, styled like the hat edge. The skirt came all the way to her knees with yet another black border, but the slits on each side both went up a good four inches. Enough room for his hand to slip inside and reach for heaven.

He'd have to remember for later.

The black heels were high enough to put her eye to eye with him, strappy things that should by all rights be falling off. He liked the black kid gloves and parasol. No one remembered old time glamour anymore. She must have talked to May Belle again because there was no way the dress wasn't vintage. But he admitted his first impression of it was wrong. It wasn't an Audrey Hepburn. It was definitely a Marilyn.

He must have been staring there for some time because he was startled by the sound of the organist tuning up. Most of the other people had finally taken seats, leaving Cass standing in the aisle looking back at him. She smiled, a wide smile filled to the brim with sensuality.

If he wasn't in love with her already, he'd have fallen right that second and not given a damn. And she knew it, the brat.

Strolling toward the front of the pews, she found an empty seat and asked if she could take it. Judging by the vast amounts of whispering, no one in the church knew who she was. Burke smiled and moved past the groomsmen lining up to go back to his seat. He passed Luke with a pat on his shoulder. "Good luck, Hanson."

"Yeah, like I need it. CB didn't even show up." Luke snickered to his friends, scuffing his feet on the carpet to dry them. "I hope you have your pink slip, Halifax."

Burke patted his breast pocket. "Right here, with Cass's name all over it." He headed back to his seat still grinning. The poor bastard would never see it coming.

Chapter Twelve

Cass locked her posture, her back straight as a board despite the temptation to slump into the pew like everyone else. People kept staring at her, most likely trying to see past her sunglasses. How funny, she grew up with most of these folks and none of them seemed to have a clue who she was. A few might have their suspicions since they'd probably seen her on her way to her practice dates at Burke's, but either they weren't talking or they hadn't put it all together yet. It was kind of nice to be the mystery woman.

What took the most control was not turning in her seat to find Burke across the church populace. It was downright painful how good he looked in his black suit, her favorite arrowhead bolo tie at his neck, standing at the front of a church while she waited in the aisle. For a full minute, she had all kinds of fantasies about walking down to meet him, getting married in front of the entire town. He didn't look terrified while he was up there, either. He looked at ease once he saw her.

And...something else.

Before she could think of what was different about him, the organist started playing the Bridal March. The sound of more than half a town rising to its feet drowned out the music for a moment before Sally began the long walk down the aisle.

Cass watched the petite woman move slowly forward with a sense of foreboding. First, Sally was barely moving. In fact, her massive yardage of white taffeta rendered her feet completely invisible, something she had a feeling the blonde was using to her best advantage. About halfway down the aisle the organist had to start the tune over and people were getting tired of standing. Sally was scouring the crowd, looking for something. No, some*one*. Desperately looking.

Cass peeled away her sunglasses, trying to catch Sally's eye, succeeding finally when she leaned outward toward the procession way. For a moment, Sally brightened, color filling her cheeks as she looked around Cass for someone else.

Hayne.

Disappointment was a sad thing to see on a bride's face. Cass put her sunglasses back on and shook her head. Sally put her eyes on the floor and finally started moving forward at regular pace. Too soon, she was at the altar next to Luke, looking small, forlorn and lost.

Cass sat with the others, most everyone grateful to be back in their seats. Guilt ate at her. Sally wasn't her friend, but a huge responsibility weighed on her all the same. She knew Sally didn't want to marry Luke. No woman in her right mind would, and though Sally was questionable in that department, even *she* was looking for a way out. The only thing stopping Cass from giving her one was a bet. A stupid bet. Sure, her reputation and her car were at stake, but at least a lifetime with Luke didn't hang in the balance.

She also had to consider her brother. For some reason, his happiness hinged on what the tiny little woman up there finally decided. Picturing Sally's lonely, lost, sullen face made Cass cringe. No, she couldn't let this wedding take place. Mentally coughing up her car keys, she put her hand on the back of the pew in front of herself and pulled herself to her feet.

The crowd gasped, whispers abounding. The pastor stopped talking and one by one, the wedding party turned around. All five of Luke's frighteningly pretty groomsmen and the flower girl at Sally's left. Cass barely recognized her as Luke's little sister, Joan. Most of them had confusion on their faces. Luke was lost for a minute but when she took off her sunglasses he flushed with triumph.

Oh, let him. It was just a car. Burke would build her another one. Sally's expression told her she'd done the right thing—she was already crying with gratefulness.

But...uh...what do I do now?

Cass turned around, finding Burke already getting to his feet to head her way. He might not be sure what she was doing but he'd stand next to her while she did it. Oh, she loved him. She opened her mouth to say so, but before she could-

"Stop this wedding!" The rifle blast to the ceiling of the church alone would have sufficed if the jackass near the doors had thought to do it before yelling and setting off double screams of shock.

Cass rolled her eyes. Only Hayne would try to pull off a kidnapping with a rifle that couldn't hit diddly if you were aiming for a hole in the ground. Even the somewhat frazzled but well-dressed older man with him was looking at him like he'd lost his mind.

"Hayne!" Sally cried. He wasn't exactly a knight in shining armor, but Cass supposed he'd do. "Daddy? Is that you?"

"Don't marry him, Sally," Cass's brother said from the back of the church, striding forward with all the heroics a rumpled guy with a day old beard and worn jeans could produce. "He's not going to keep his promise."

"What promise?" Cass asked out of sheer curiosity before realizing she was probably ruining his big romantic interruption.

Hayne spared her a glance. "Sally wants to move to a small town, live like regular people, like us. It's her dream. Her father is a movie producer. She's lived her whole life like a doll, practically living one of her dad's movies. Luke promised to bring her here to live after they got married, but he's not going to, sweetheart," Hayne said softly, turning his eyes back to Sally.

Sally eyes filled with tears while she trembled near the altar and the church rippled with gasps of juicy gossip.

"How'd you find out?" Cass asked, knowing she'd missed something.

"That's where I went last night. I was going to go up to the cabin and pretend this wedding wasn't happening. Instead, I drove up to Hollywood and beat down the gates to Sally's father's house. She told me how hurt she was that he wouldn't break his meetings to give her away." Hayne slid the older man a dirty look.

"I would have been there for the scheduled wedding. There wasn't time to clear another whole day on such short notice," Sally's father replied, no doubt taking in the accusing glares from everyone around him. The disapproving grumbles would be hard to miss.

"You're marrying the wrong guy, Sally," Hayne interjected, taking another step toward her. "We started talking on the drive back here. Your father can tell you, Luke doesn't plan to come home. He's got contracts already to star in two movies overseas. Tell her!"

"It's true, dear. I thought you knew. It's been in the works for a few months now." Sally's father ignored the crowd, speaking directly to his daughter with a gentle compassion that made Cass a touch more willing to forgive him. Whether Sally would remained to be seen. "When your young man here told me you were getting married today thinking you'd have a home here, I understood why you were so hurt. Luke said you'd agreed to put off settling down. I thought you were getting married here for his parents' sake and the real wedding would take place in Brentwood as planned. I would never miss your wedding day."

Sally turned to Luke, her blushed cheeks turning dark for another reason all together. "You *what?*"

Luke swallowed, his apologetic mask already in place. "Now, now, sweetie, don't be upset. It was a once in a lifetime opportunity. I had to take it! It was my big break!"

"Your big break? Break to *what?* I thought you were tired of begging for work, of never knowing where your next gig would be. You said you wanted to come home!"

"We are home. For now…"

"And what was I supposed to do while you were having your big break? Follow you around like some kind of…of…"

"Pomeranian," Cass supplied.

"Pomeranian!" Sally snapped up the word and shoved her perfect bouquet into Luke's chest. "You lied to me! You said we were going to have it all!"

"We will have it all. Fame, fortune, a future."

"A *lie!*" Sally huffed. Cass covered her mouth with her fingertips, surprised. The Pomeranian had bite. "That's not the future I want, Luke Hanson. Not now, not ever. This wedding is off!"

People probably shouldn't have cheered, but they did. Sally stomped down the few steps to the bridal pathway where Hayne waited.

"*You* did this!" Luke accused, pointing at Cass and bringing everything to a halt.

Her eyebrows rose. "Me? What did I do?"

"What *didn't* you do? First you and Halifax tell the entire town I'm gay when you know I'm not. You break my nose and then you get me wrapped up in this bet so your brother can steal my bride! As if that wasn't enough, your friend peed on my shoes!"

If she didn't know better, she'd think Luke was about to cry. Cass looked up at Burke. "Peed?"

"More of a leak," he amended with a blasé nod of his head. "I'll tell you later."

"Do me a favor and don't."

"Damn it, CB, this isn't a joke!" Luke's golden coloring mottled into an unbecoming purple.

Cass couldn't bring herself to care. "No, it's not, Luke. You've now blown two weddings in the same church because you're a self-centered jerk who never once thinks about his actions or how they'll affect the people he claims he loves. I'm sure it will make you a great movie star but it's not going to do anything for you here. I hope you're happy overseas, Luke, I really do. I just hope you don't come home again until you grow up. "

"CB," Luke growled it like a swear word.

"Excuse me!" Hayne yelled, interrupting the oncoming tantrum. "I'm in the middle of something here, if you don't mind! Still the madman with a gun, people!"

"Sorry," Cass mumbled.

"It's okay." He shrugged, facing the front again, where Sally waited at the first pew, smiling the way a bride should. "Sally, I know it's been a fast relationship. I know you'll think I'm crazy, but when I thought about how easily I might be losing you because I didn't take the initiative, I knew there was no way I'd ask you to leave this wedding if I couldn't ask you to come to ours." He kneeled right there in the aisle next to Cass's pew. "Marry me, Sally. We'll settle down right here in RDC and have all those kids you kept talking about. We'll find our dreams together."

The whole church turned to Sally in her mile-of-white dress, wiping tears off her face.

"Please, Sally?" Hayne reached out his hand.

She came running.

"Hey! What about me?" Luke yelled.

"Marry one of the groomsmen," she called over her shoulder.

Just before catching his soon-to-be bride, Hayne tossed the hunting rifle to Cass. "Go use it on Burke. Looks like the damn thing's lucky."

To her utter shock—*oh, God, Sally is going to be a member of my family!*—her brother ran off with the bride, yelling behind him to have the pastor bill him for the damages. Sally blew a kiss to her father and they were gone. Cass watched them go, her eyes stinging with what suspiciously felt like tears.

"Oh, this is the most romantic thing I think I've ever seen!" the woman next to her exclaimed, setting off assenting murmurs throughout the church.

Great. Hayne Bishop, *Romantic God.* She'd never hear the end of it.

"I don't think you'll be needing this," Burke's deep voice rumbled in her ear, sending shivers run down her spine as he plucked the useless rifle from her hands. "It doesn't quite match your dress."

"I don't know, worked for Hayne." He was so close that if she pursed her lips she'd taste him. It sounded like a good idea.

"Trust me, sweetheart, you're dangerous enough." Then in front of God, pastor and town, he kissed her, tongue and everything.

Cass could have stood there forever, lost in the bliss of Burke's kiss, but there was a thud and the bliss turned to a bang. Jumping back, she realized the rifle had fallen, firing on contact. Looking to the altar, she quickly counted five groomsmen but no groom.

"Ah, hell!" Burke rushed to the front, pulling Cass along with him until they got to where Luke lay on the altar steps, unconscious.

"Oh my God! Did we shoot him?" She checked him for blood, holes, anything, but found nothing more than a crisp tuxedo shirt.

"Christ!" The pastor's voice rang out in holy terror, distracting them and sending the guests into paroxysms of shock. "You shot the statue of Christ!"

Sure enough, the poor statue's toe was missing, along with a nice chunk of the wood stand it was on. Cass looked from the statue to the man she was kneeling next to. "It missed him?"

"Looks like," Burke said, his voice a little tight. "I think maybe he fainted."

Cass realized after a few seconds he was trying not to laugh. "The rifle *was* pointed at him, Burke."

He shrugged, his smile growing.

"It's not polite to laugh at the weak."

Those dimples he hated showed as he ducked his head to stifle his chuckles.

"Could be worse," she couldn't resist teasing. "He might have wet himself."

His loud bark of laughter was enough to make her happy for a week. People were starting to mill around again, some leaving, their whispers making a low roar in the building. She stood up and reached a hand down to him. "Come on, let's blow this pop stand before he comes to and figures out he won the bet."

"But Cass—"

As he was taking her hand, the church doors burst open and paramedics arrived in a fluster, shocking some of the guests yet again. Most likely, the pastor would be removing those things before the next wedding.

"Did we hear gunshots?" The first one in asked, looking around.

"That was fast," Cass muttered. "Over here. He probably gave himself a concussion on the steps."

"Back there," Burke redirected, pointing to the door at the back of the church. "Woman in labor."

"What about this guy?" The two men paused momentarily to take a look at Luke.

"He's all right, head's harder than a rock. He only fainted, anyway." Burke got up so one of the EMTs could inspect Luke while the other went back to the office. Cass wondered how much control it took for Burke not to kick Luke where he lay.

"Is Alice back there?" she asked, once they were free of Luke's limp limbs. People were talking louder now around them, some sending congratulations to her on their way out, though she wasn't sure what for. Probably to pass on to Hayne.

Burke nodded in answer to her question. "She thought she had more time."

"She's going to be mad she missed this," Cass smiled, wondering if she'd be able to describe what had happened to Alice's satisfaction. With any luck, someone had it on tape.

"We'll make it up to her at our wedding," he said matter-of-factly, fitting her hand to his.

Cass, startled, looked up at him. "Did you say *our* wedding?"

He pretended to think about it. She shoved at his shoulder, making him laugh. "It sounded like it, didn't it?"

"You're supposed to *ask*, Halifax."

"Why? We both know it's inevitable."

Funny how hopes can be dashed so quickly. "The only thing inevitable was me realizing—"

"How much I love you," he said softly, suddenly more serious than she'd ever seen him in her life. For cutting her off, it wasn't too bad of an interruption.

"I thought you said you weren't built that way."

"I didn't think I was." A trembling thumb brushed her cheek. "You're not the only one who's changed the last few weeks, Cassie."

She captured his hand, holding it close to her face. Part of her wanted to close her eyes, to savor this moment. The smart parts kept them open, so she could see it and remember it for the rest of her life.

"I never meant to hurt you. It's not easy getting your eyes opened. But mine have been."

"Say it again," she whispered, closing her eyes to savor it. "So I can believe it."

"I love you, Cassandra Bishop. Have from the first time I saw you. I just didn't know it. It wasn't because you dressed yourself up, either. You have no idea how hard it was not making love to you that day you stood up in my bathtub. Wanting you has nothing to do with Luke, your dresses or anything else you do to yourself. I love you. I want to be with you, however you feel like dressing or acting, for the rest of our lives. I know I didn't figure it out until you were gone, but that's when I realized it was always there. Just like you said."

"Are you saying I was right and you were wrong?"

His eyelid twitched. "Why don't I just say I can't wait to marry you?"

She raised her brow. "That's not asking, Burke."

"I haven't changed *that* much." He tugged on her hands to start her walking down the aisle again. "When do you want to do this thing?"

"Well, I *am* all dressed up with nowhere to go."

"Elope?" He raised his eyebrows. "Today? What about your family?"

"Hayne's off with someone else's bride and Dad's doing who knows what with Lola Velasquez," she reminded. "Trust me, no one will mind."

"What if *I* mind? Don't you want the whole town at *your* wedding?"

She considered the fallen plaster, the fainted groom, the puddle of whatever that was in the aisle and…yes, that was a baby screaming somewhere back there. She looked at him pointedly.

He pulled her to his side. "I guess we elope."

"Hey, Burke, you want this now?" Billy, one of Burke's garage guys, held a bucket full of money, carrying it as if it weighed a ton.

Cass frowned. "What's this?"

"It's the bar pool. Used to be the garage pool, but the boss made us move it. Anyways, here's your winnings." He handed Burke the bucket while Cass stared at all the money. "There'd be more but after you came in and put the two hundred down, the Panyons and the Butners figured it was okay to bet and joined you."

"You bet against me?" She pulled her hand from him, stung. Luke hadn't lied? Oh, that hurt. "*All* of you bet against me?"

"*Against* you?" Billy laughed as if she'd made a joke. "All of them bet you'd have Luke down on his knees apologizing. We figured out on his ass was just as good."

"Billy?" Burke growled.

"Yeah, boss?"

"Go hand out the other winnings, will you?"

"Sure," he replied obliviously. "Congrats, CB! By the way, you look great! I was wondering—"

"Billy!"

The young man jumped at Burke's bark, waving briefly before casually running for his life.

Cass blinked at the money bucket, bewildered. "But I lost!"

"You did? When? When you showed up looking like the sexiest, most untouchable woman on earth? Or when you were the only one to get that poor kid out of her mess with Luke? Maybe when you stood up for yourself in front of everybody and told Luke exactly what he really was?"

"But…but—" Cass tried to come up with the way she'd lost. She knew she had…hadn't she? "I'm still not much of a lady, Burke. This is all a show." She rubbed the dress indicatively.

"Yup, it is." They got to the doors before he smiled down at her. "You've always been a lady, Cass. Turns out none of *us* were smart enough to know it."

"It's a boy!" Sel yelled from the back of the church, laughing and whooping to the cheers and grumbles of many in the crowd.

Cass watched even more fives and ones exchange hands. "Is this whole town a gambling hall?"

"Right down to the last cowboy boot." Burke grinned. They finally made it outside, past all the noise and excitement. They walked along the sidewalk leading to the parking lot. .

"Where should we go?" Town Hall didn't exactly fill her head with hearts and flowers.

Burke thought a minute, slowing his steps to a standstill. "Considering we have a bucket of money and we're a pair of notorious gamblers, I'd say there's only one place to go—Vegas, baby."

She scrunched her face. The land of gaudy lights, plastic Elvises and all night dollar buffets? "*Las* Vegas?"

"Is there another kind?"

"It's a little glitzy isn't it?"

"Where else should betting hearts get hitched?"

"Are you getting romantic in your old age, Halifax?" She smiled up at him, getting excited. It didn't matter where they got married. Their future waited, just a few steps away.

"No," he replied, matter of fact, "but I bet it happens eventually."

Cass laughed. "You would."

He stopped them, stepping forward and carefully offering his hand. "Ready for anything, Cassie?"

His eyes glowed down at her, full of everything she ever dreamed possible and more. So much more. She put her hand in his without a second thought.

"I always am, Burke. I always am."

Dee Tenorio

Dee Tenorio is a sick woman. Really sick. She enjoys tormenting herself by writing romantic comedies (preferably with sexy, grumpy heroes and smart-mouthed heroines) and sizzling, steamy romances of various genres spanning dramas with the occasional drop of suspense all the way to erotic romances. But why does that make her sick?

Because she truly seems to enjoy it.

And she has every intention of keeping at it!

If you would like to learn more about Dee and her work, please visit her website at www.deetenorio.com.

Visit Dee's blog: http://www.deetenorio.com/Blog

Coming Soon from Dee Tenario

Midnight Sonata, first in the Midnight Trilogy – September '06
Midnight Temptation, Midnight Trilogy book 2 – December '06

Samhain Publishing, Ltd.

It's all about the story…

Action/Adventure
Fantasy
Historical
Horror
Mainstream
Mystery/Suspense
Non-Fiction
Paranormal
Red Hots!
Romance
Science Fiction
Western
Young Adult

http://www.samhainpublishing.com

Printed in the United States
57679LVS00005B/139-969